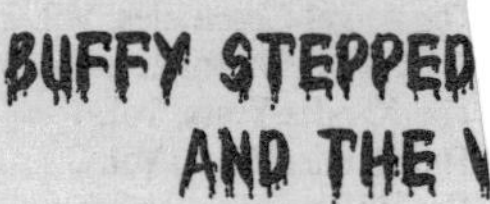

"You know, I just wanted to start over. Be like everybody else. Have some friends, maybe a dog. . . . But no. You had to come here. You couldn't go suck on some other town."

Before Buffy could go on, a voice came from the shadows behind her. "You're wasting my time," Luke said calmly.

"Hey," Buffy retorted, "I had other plans, too, okay?"

The vampire shoved a heavy stone slab straight at her, but Buffy leaped over it and jumped on top. With one swift movement, she flipped over and planted both feet solidly on Luke's chest. The momentum caused both of them to fall, but Buffy managed to get up first, pulling out her stake and driving it toward his chest. Luke's hand shot out and grabbed it just before it made contact.

"You think you can stop me?" Luke's face was twisted with rage. "Stop us?" He squeezed his fist. The stake splintered like a matchstick.

Victorious now, he loomed over her, contemplating her with gleeful animal hunger.

Buffy the Vampire Slayer™

Buffy the Vampire Slayer (movie tie-in)
The Harvest
Halloween Rain
Coyote Moon
Night of the Living Rerun
Blooded
Visitors
Unnatural Selection
Power of Persuasion
Deep Water
Here Be Monsters
Ghoul Trouble
Doomsday Deck
The Angel Chronicles, Vol. 1
The Angel Chronicles, Vol. 2
The Angel Chronicles, Vol. 3
The Xander Years, Vol. 1
The Xander Years, Vol. 2
The Willow Files, Vol. 1
The Willow Files, Vol. 2
How I Survived My Summer Vacation, Vol. 1

Available from ARCHWAY Paperbacks and POCKET PULSE

Buffy the Vampire Slayer adult books

Child of the Hunt
Return to Chaos
The Gatekeeper Trilogy
  Book 1: Out of the Madhouse
  Book 2: Ghost Roads
  Book 3: Sons of Entropy
Obsidian Fate
Immortal
Sins of the Father
Resurrecting Ravana
Prime Evil
The Evil That Men Do
Paleo
Spike and Dru: Pretty Maids All in a Row
Revenant

The Watcher's Guide, Vol. 1: The Official Companion to the Hit Show
The Watcher's Guide, Vol. 2: The Official Companion to the Hit Show
The Postcards
The Essential Angel
The Sunnydale High Yearbook
Buffy the Vampire Slayer: Pop Quiz
The Monster Book
The Script Book, Season One Vol. 1
The Script Book, Season One Vol. 2

Available from POCKET BOOKS

THE HARVEST

A novelization by Richie Tankersley Cusick
Based on the episodes by Joss Whedon • Created by Joss Whedon

POCKET PULSE
New York London Toronto Sydney Singapore

An *Original* Publication of POCKET BOOKS

POCKET PULSE, published by
Pocket Books, a division of Simon & Schuster, Inc.
1230 Avenue of the Americas, New York, NY 10020

ISBN: 0-671-01712-8

First Pocket Pulse printing September 1997

15 14 13 12 11 10 9

POCKET PULSE and colophon are registered trademarks of Simon & Schuster, Inc.

Cover photo by James Sorenson

Printed in the U.S.A.

IL: 7+

to Frances Wenner with love
for teaching me how to slay
all those creatures of the dark

Virginia, 1866: The frequent disappearance of local Civil War widows shocked an already grieving community. These events ended when Lucy Hanover arrived in town.

Chicago, May 1927: Forty-one bodies were found near Union Station. Shortly after the arrival of a certain young woman, the mysterious murders stopped.

FOR EACH GENERATION
THERE IS ONLY ONE SLAYER

Now it's starting all over again. . . .

THE HARVEST

Prologue

Sunnydale High School looked different at night.

In fact, it looked almost scary.

Classes had been over for hours, and now the buildings lay empty and eerily silent, walls gleaming dark in the moonlight. Shadows clung to the stairwells; rooms gaped along the corridors like so many abandoned caves. When a window suddenly shattered inside one of them, the echo seemed to hang there forever, even as a hand thrust beyond the broken glass, fumbling with the lock and sliding the window up.

"Are you sure this is a good idea?"

The girl who spoke looked around nervously as her male companion climbed through, then reached back to help her.

"It's a great idea!" he insisted. "Come on."

He led her out into the hallway. It was even

blacker out here than the classroom had been, and the girl threw him a timid glance.

"You go to school here?"

"Used to," he said. "On top of the gym, it's so cool—you can see the whole town."

"I don't want to go up there."

His body moved against hers. "Oh, you can't wait, huh?"

"We're just gonna get in trouble," she protested, but he only pressed closer.

"Count on it."

As he kissed her, he felt the tensing of her shoulders, felt her pull away from him, saw the genuine look of fear upon her face.

"What was that?"

"What was what?" he asked impatiently.

"I heard a noise."

"It's nothing."

"Maybe it's something . . ."

"Maybe it's some Thing . . ." he deadpanned.

"That's not funny."

Grudgingly the boy surveyed their surroundings. The hall was still dark, still completely deserted, yet the shadows seemed to have thickened somehow, creeping up on them while they hadn't been watching. He could feel the girl cowering close behind him.

"Hello . . ." he called softly, teasingly.

Silence.

"There's nobody here," he said at last, turning back to her.

But she still sounded frightened. “Are you sure?”

“I’m sure.”

“Okay,” she murmured.

And then, as her face contorted into a horrible shape, she bared her fangs, burying them swiftly into his neck.

CHAPTER 1

Buffy was lost.

Wandering through a place she didn't know and didn't want to know.

A subterranean chamber, perhaps, or the hidden lair of some horrible beast—this dark, forgotten place of dampness and decay. She moved on through the gloom, wary and confused, trying to figure out where she was, how to find her way out again. And yet while one small part of her mind *knew* she was dreaming—*had* to be dreaming—another part warned her that this place was all too real, all too horribly close.

Images jumped out at her, then faded again almost instantly, leaving only the vaguest of memories in their wake. She saw candles flickering over a deep red pool . . . clawing fingers through a glow of fire . . . drawings of beasts and the silvery glint of a cross. Demonic laughter echoed among crumbling headstones—faceless figures stalked her—and then suddenly, startlingly clear, she saw a book, a very old book with the word *VAMPYR* engraved upon its cover . . .

From far, far away she could feel herself tossing and turning upon her bed, tossing and struggling even as the dream pulled her deeper and deeper into its spell. Without warning a shadow rose up behind her, foul and evil, a shadow black as death, roaring through her head, through her veins—*"I'll take you . . . like a cancer . . . I'll get inside you and eat my way out—"*

Buffy's eyes flew open.

Even in the light of morning, it was as if the nightmare still lingered, the horror of it, the danger of it . . .

She sat up in bed, blinking against the brightness that streamed in through her window. She was awake now; she was perfectly safe. This was her room . . . her house . . . her reality—

"Buffy?"

"I'm up, Mom."

"Don't want to be late for your first day!" Joyce Summers called from the hallway.

"No," Buffy mumbled to herself. "Wouldn't want that."

She heard the uncertainty in her own voice. She sat up and stared around the room, at the half-decorated walls, the unpacked boxes stacked in one corner.

Then with a sigh, she forced the last dregs of nightmare from her mind and got up to face the day.

"Now, you have a good time," Joyce Summers said, watching Buffy get out of the car. "I know you'll make friends right away. Think positive. And, honey . . ." she paused, sounding hopeful. "Try not to get kicked out."

"I promise."

As her mother drove off, Buffy stood for a moment, sizing up her new situation. The weather this morning was Southern California-perfect, and throngs of students were laughing and talking as they crammed their way leisurely into Sunnydale High. *Well . . . might as well get this over with.*

Sighing, Buffy started in, so deep in her thoughts that she didn't notice the cute boy on the skateboard.

"Coming through . . ." Xander announced, weaving his way recklessly through the crowds. "Coming through . . . not certain how to stop . . ."

He was tall and dark-haired, with a look of shaggy indifference about him, and as he headed toward the entrance, he suddenly spied a girl he'd never seen before.

She was short and petite, with dark blond hair and big blue eyes, and her face had that heart-shaped cuteness that he never could resist. She was wearing boots and a really short skirt, and as Xander passed her he craned his neck for a better view and completely forgot about navigating.

At the last possible second he managed to miss the steps, but only by ducking beneath a railing. He landed in a heap on the pavement, and as a familiar face ran up to help him, he looked at her with a grin that was all charm.

"Willow!" Xander exclaimed, picking himself up again, not at all bothered by his dramatic entrance. "You're so very much the person I wanted to see."

"Really?" Willow asked hopefully.

She was considered plain and totally boring by Sunnydale standards; it was bad enough that her nose was always buried in some book, but even worse were the rumors that her mother actually picked out her clothes. Yet a keen intelligence shone in Willow's soft brown eyes, and her smile was poignantly sweet—and as Xander came toward her now, she brightened at his attention. Xander, as usual, didn't seem to notice.

"Yeah," he said. "You know, I kind of had a problem with the math."

Willow quickly hid her disappointment. "Which part?"

"The math. Can you help me tonight? Please? Be my study buddy?"

"Well," Willow considered cheerfully, "what's in it for me?"

"A shiny nickel . . ."

"Okay. Do you have *Theories in Trig?* You should check it out."

Xander looked baffled. "Check it out?"

"From the library. Where the books live."

"Right." He grinned again. "I'm there. See, I *want* to change."

As they went inside and pushed their way along the packed corridor, they saw their friend Jesse approaching.

"Hey," Jesse nodded, and Xander raised his arm in a casual wave.

"Jesse! What's what?"

Jesse didn't hesitate. "New girl!"

"That's right," Xander confirmed enthusiastically. "I saw her. She's pretty much a hottie."

"I heard someone was transferring here," Willow added.

"So," Xander insisted. "Tell."

"Tell what?" Jesse asked. He was tall and gangly with short-cropped hair and thick brows. Definitely not one of the hot guys at Sunnydale.

"What's the sitch?" Xander urged. "What do you know about her?"

Jesse shrugged matter-of-factly. "New girl."

"Well," Xander came back at him without missing a beat. "You're certainly a font of nothing."

Buffy sat in the principal's office, across the desk from Mr. Flutie. He was middle-aged and overweight, slightly impressed with his own importance, she noted. As she watched him, he pulled her transcript from a folder, glanced through it, then turned a direct gaze on her.

"Buffy Summers," he recited. "Sophomore, late of Hemery High in Los Angeles. Interesting record. Quite a career."

Before Buffy could answer, he smiled and carefully tore her transcript into four pieces.

"Welcome to Sunnydale," he announced. "A clean slate, Buffy, that's what you get here. What's past is past. We're not interested in what it says on a piece of paper. Even if it says—" He broke off and looked down again at the ripped pages. His eyes went wide. "Whoa. At Sunnydale we nurture the whole student. The inner student."

Having recovered himself, Mr. Flutie continued to talk while picking up the pieces of her transcript and arranging them back into their original shape.

"Other schools might look at the incredible decline in grade point average," he went on. "We look at the struggling young *woman* with the incredible decline in grade point average. Other schools might look at the reports of gang fights—"

"Mr. Flutie—" Buffy interrupted.

"All the kids here are free to call me Bob—"

"Bob—"

"But they don't."

He pulled out a piece of tape and began taping the transcript together again.

"Mr. Flutie. I know my transcripts are a little . . . colorful—"

"Hey, we're not caring about that! Do you think 'colorful' is the word? Not 'dismal'? Just offhand, I'd go with 'dismal.' "

"It wasn't that bad."

Mr. Flutie stared at her. "You burned down the gym."

"I did. I really did." Buffy winced. "But you gotta see the big picture. I mean the gym was full of vamp . . . uh, asbestos."

"Buffy. Don't worry. Any other school, they might say 'Watch your step,' or 'We'll be watching you,' or 'Get within a hundred yards of the gym with a book of matches and you'll grow up in juvie hall,' but that's just not the way here. We want to service your needs and help you to respect our needs. And if your needs and our needs don't mesh . . ."

Still smiling blandly, he slipped the messily mended transcript back into her folder and slammed it shut with his hand. Buffy jumped, her own forced smile going doubtful.

She felt depressed as she left Mr. Flutie's office. As she paused there in the hallway, rummaging through her bag, a distracted student bumped into her, sending her stuff flying in all directions. Frustrated, Buffy knelt down and started scooping everything back up. For the second time that morning she failed to see Xander, who was standing close by and had witnessed the whole incident. Immediately he came over and knelt beside her.

"Can I have you," Xander asked, then corrected himself. "Dyeh—can I help you?"

"Oh, thanks."

He started picking up her things and handing them to her.

"I don't know you, do I?"

"I'm new. I'm Buffy."

"Xander. Is me. Hi."

"Thanks."

"Maybe I'll see you around," Xander suggested. "Maybe at school, since we both . . . go there."

"Great. Nice to meet you."

He gave her the rest of her books. She stuffed them into her bag and hurried away.

" 'We both go to school,' " Xander shook his head in disgust. "Very suave. Very not pathetic."

Then he noticed something on the floor. Bending down to retrieve it, he automatically called after her, "Oh, hey, you forgot your—"

He broke off. He looked at the thing he was holding.

"Stake," he said.

Buffy was too far away now to hear him.

With a puzzled frown, Xander stared at the wooden stake clutched in his hand.

CHAPTER 2

Buffy sat in the back of her history class, earnestly taking notes. The teacher's voice droned on and on while she tried to keep up.

"It's estimated that about twenty-five million people died in that one four-year span. But the fun part of the Black Plague is that it originated in Europe: How? As an early form of germ warfare. The plague was first found in Asia, and a Kipchak army actually catapulted plague-infested corpses into a Genoise trading post. Ingenious. If you look at the map on page sixty-three you can trace the spread of the disease . . ."

Everyone opened their books. Buffy didn't have one yet, and as she looked around at the other kids, a girl in the desk next to hers leaned over. She was tall and very pretty in an exotic sort of way, obviously self-assured, and was wearing a killer outfit of tight pants and a mostly see-through shirt.

"Here," the girl said. She moved her book so Buffy could share it.

"Thanks," Buffy smiled.

"And this popular plague led to what social changes?" the teacher continued. Buffy thought class would never end. When the bell rang at last, the girl finally introduced herself.

"Hi, I'm Cordelia."

"I'm Buffy."

"If you're looking for a textbook of your very own, there's probably a few in the library."

"Oh, great. Thanks. Where would that be?"

"I'll show you."

The girls walked out into the crowded hall and Cordelia glanced at Buffy with unconcealed interest.

"You transferred from Hemery, right? In L.A.?"

"Yeah."

"Oh! I would kill to live in L.A. Being that close to that many shoes . . . Why'd you come here?"

"Because my mom moved, is the reason. I mean, we both moved. But my mom wanted to."

"Well, you'll be okay here," Cordelia assured her. "If you hang with me and mine, you'll be accepted in no time. Of course, we do have to test your coolness factor. You're from L.A., so you can skip the written, but let's see . . . Vamp nail polish."

Buffy asked tentatively, "Over?"

"So over," Cordelia replied. "James Spader."

"He *needs* to call me."

"Frappachinos?"

"Trendy but tasty."

"John Tesh."

"The Devil?"

Cordelia nodded. "Well, that was pretty much a gimme, but you passed."

"Oh, good." Buffy put a hand to her heart in mock relief.

They stopped at the water fountain, where Willow was taking her turn.

"Willow!" Cordelia raised a perfectly plucked eyebrow. "Nice dress. Good to know you've seen the softer side of Sears."

Buffy saw the instant hurt on Willow's face. She stared at Cordelia, surprised by the girl's sudden viciousness.

Willow sounded almost apologetic. "Well, my mom picked it out."

"No wonder you're such a guy magnet." Cordelia's tone was withering. "Are you done?"

"Oh," Willow said softly, instantly vacating the fountain. Cordelia stepped up to it and glanced at Buffy.

"You wanna fit in here, the first rule is, 'Know your losers.' Once you can identify them all by sight, they're a lot easier to avoid."

She bent down to drink. Buffy looked unhappily at the departing Willow, then followed Cordelia on to the library.

"And if you're not too swamped with catching up, you should come out to the Bronze tonight," Cordelia suggested.

"The who?"

"The Bronze. It's the only club worth going to around here. They let anybody in, but it's still the scene. It's in the bad part of town."

"Where's that?" Buffy asked.

"About half a block from the good part of town. We don't have a whole lot of town. You should show."

They'd reached the library now. The two of them stopped in front of the door.

"Well, I'll try, thanks," Buffy promised.

"Good. I'll see you at gym and you can tell me absolutely everything there is to know about yourself."

Cordelia turned and went off. Buffy, slightly thrown off by the idea of giving her whole life story, allowed herself an ironic smile.

"That sounds like fun," she mumbled.

She entered the library, surprised at the elegance of it, the dark wood paneling, the streaming sunlight across the floor, the shelves and shelves of books. A short flight of stairs led up to a second level of still more bookcases, and with its large oak table and cozy study lamps, the room had a curiously warm country-house feeling.

There didn't seem to be anyone around. As she paused beside the checkout counter, she happened to notice a folded newspaper lying there, an article on its first page circled in red. The headline stated "Local Boys Still Missing," and beside it was a blurry picture of three boys.

Buffy wandered farther in. She peered around a bookcase.

"Hello . . . is anybody here?"

Without warning someone touched her shoulder. Startled, she spun to face him.

"Can I help you?" the man asked politely. He spoke with a British accent, and his expression was one of quiet intensity.

Buffy breathed a sigh of relief. "I was looking for some, well, books. I'm new."

"Miss Summers," the man said.

"Good call. I guess I'm the only new kid."

"I'm Mr. Giles, the librarian."

Buffy studied him for an instant. Tall, slender, with a refined sort of elegance, dressed in English tweeds and wools, a pinstripe shirt and tie. Kind eyes stared back at her from behind thin wire-rimmed glasses.

"Great." Buffy smiled. "So you have, uh—"

"I know what you're after."

He turned and led her to the checkout desk by the door. Buffy could see his office just behind it, but Mr. Giles obviously hadn't meant to take her there. She watched curiously as he pulled a book out from beneath the counter and slid it toward her. Huge and leather bound, it bore a single word in gilt upon its cover.

VAMPYR

It was the book from her nightmare.

Concern flooded Buffy's face—and with it, a look of wary understanding. She stepped back from the desk, but her gaze remained on the librarian.

"That's not what I'm looking for," she told him, her voice going tight.

"Are you sure?"

"I'm way sure."

Mr. Giles hesitated . . . gave an almost imperceptible nod. "My mistake."

He replaced the book under the counter.

"So," he continued softly, "what is it you said—"

He stared out into the empty room.

Buffy had gone.

At almost the same moment Buffy left the library, two other students happened to be discussing her while they changed their clothes in the girls' locker room.

"The new kid?" one girl said. "She seems kind of weird to me. And what kind of name is Buffy?"

She turned as another friend called to her. "Hey, Aphrodesia."

"Hey," she said distractedly.

"Well," Aura said, picking up the conversation. "The chatter in the caf is that she got kicked out of her last school, and that's why her mom had to get a new job."

"Neg," Aphrodesia replied, but Aura nodded.

"Pos. She was starting fights."

Aphrodesia opened her locker. "Negly!"

"Well, I heard it from Blue," Aura insisted, tugging open her own door, "and she saw the transcripts—"

She never got to finish the sentence.

Without warning something flew out of the locker, and Aphrodesia screamed as the body of a dead boy collapsed on top of her. His eyes were wide and staring, as though they had witnessed something truly horrible. She didn't recognize him, and she had no way of knowing that he'd broken into the school with his girlfriend last night, with the romantic intention of going up to the roof of the gym.

All she could do was keep on screaming as the body sprawled at her feet, gazing up at her from the floor.

CHAPTER 3

Willow carefully sorted through her packed lunch. Healthy as usual. And totally boring. She was so involved that she didn't notice anyone approaching until a voice spoke behind her.

"Uh, hi," the voice said. "Willow, right?"

Willow started and turned around. "Why?" she asked suspiciously, and then, seeing who it was, "I mean, hi. Did you want me to move?"

"Why don't we start with 'Hi, I'm Buffy,' " Buffy suggested, sitting down beside her. "And then let's segue directly into me asking you for a favor. It doesn't involve moving, but it does involve you hanging out with me for a while."

Willow's expression was doubtful. "But aren't you . . . hanging with Cordelia?"

"I can't do both?"

"Not legally."

"Look, I really want to get by here," Buffy explained. "New school . . . Cordelia's been really nice—to me, anyway—but I have this burning desire not to flunk all my classes, and I heard a rumor that you were the person to talk to if I wanted to get caught up."

Willow brightened. "Oh, I could totally help you out! If you have sixth period free, we could meet in the library—"

"Or not," Buffy declined at once. "Or, you know, we could meet somewhere quieter. Louder. That place kind of gives me a wiggins."

"It has that effect on most kids. I love it, though. It's a great collection, and the new librarian's really cool."

"He's new?"

"Yeah, he just started. He was a curator of some British museum. Or *the* British Museum, I'm not sure. But he knows everything and he brought all these historical volumes and biographies, and am I the single dullest person alive?"

"Not at all!" Buffy insisted.

The girls looked up as Xander sauntered over with Jesse.

"Hey. Are you guys busy?" Xander greeted them. "Can we interrupt? We're interrupting."

"Hey," Buffy smiled.

"Hey there," Jesse answered.

"Buffy, this is Jesse." Willow made the introductions. "And that's Xander."

"Oh, me and Buffy go way back," Xander said

casually. "Old friends, very close. Then there was that period of estrangement, I think we were both changing as people, but here we are, and it's like old times, I'm quite moved."

Buffy stared at him half amused, half amazed.

"Is it me?" Jesse asked him. "Or are you turning into a babbling idiot?"

For a split second Xander looked almost embarrassed. "It's not you."

"It's nice to meet you guys," Buffy said. "I think."

"Well, we wanted to welcome you, make you feel at home," Jesse replied gallantly. "Unless you have a scary home."

"And to return this," Xander added. He produced the stake that had fallen earlier from Buffy's bag. "The only thing I can figure is that you're building a really little fence."

"Oh. No." Buffy's mind worked swiftly. "That was for self-defense. Everyone has them in L.A. Pepper spray is so passé."

Xander nodded, as though not quite convinced. "So. What do you like, what do you do for fun, what do you look for in a man? . . . Let's hear it."

"If you have any dark, painful secrets that we could publish," Jesse suggested.

"Gee," Buffy's tone was mildly sarcastic. "Everybody wants to know about me. How keen."

"Well, not a lot happens in a one-Starbucks town like Sunnydale," Xander confessed. "You're big news."

"I'm not. Really."

"Are these people bothering you?" Cordelia suddenly appeared behind Jesse, a look of pure disdain on her face.

Buffy glanced around in surprise. "Oh! No."

"She's not hanging out with us," Willow hastened to explain, while Jesse only looked smitten at the sight of her.

"Hey, Cordelia," Jesse said.

"Oh, please," Cordelia dismissed him in disgust, turning her attention to Buffy. "I don't want to interrupt your downward mobility. I just thought I'd tell you that you won't be meeting Coach Foster, the woman with chest hair, because gym has been canceled due to the extreme dead guy in the locker."

Buffy stared at her. "What?"

"What are you talking about?" Willow straightened, looking alarmed.

"Some guy was stuffed in Aura's locker," Cordelia explained.

"Dead," Buffy repeated.

"Way dead," Cordelia confirmed.

"So not just a little dead, then," Xander added.

Cordelia gave him one of her looks. "Don't you have an elsewhere to be?"

"If you need a shoulder to cry on," Jesse offered, "or just to nibble on—"

"How did he die?" Buffy broke in, her gaze still steady upon Cordelia.

"I don't know . . ."

"Well, were there any marks?"

"Morbid much?" Cordelia was eyeing her as though she were some kind of alien. "I didn't ask!"

Abruptly Buffy stood up. "Uh, look, I gotta book. I'll see you guys later."

"What's her deal?" Cordelia asked, sounding annoyed.

Buffy took off hurriedly toward the gym, leaving the others to stare after her in bewilderment.

Chapter 4

Buffy went straight to the girls' locker room. Unfortunately, Mr. Flutie was just coming out, closing the door behind him.

"Oh! Buffy!" He regarded her in surprise. "Uh, what do you want?"

Buffy tried to keep her voice casual. "Um, is there a guy in there who's dead?"

"Where did you hear that?" Mr. Flutie asked quickly. Then, "Okay. Yes. But he's not a student! Not currently."

"Do you know how he died?"

"What?"

"I mean," Buffy fumbled, "how could this have happened?"

"Well, that's for the police to determine when they get here," Mr. Flutie replied. "But this structure is safe, we have inspections, and I think there's no grounds for a lawsuit."

"Was there a lot of blood?" Buffy couldn't help asking. "Was there *any* blood?"

Mr. Flutie gave her a long look. "I would think you wouldn't want to involve yourself in this kind of thing."

"I don't," Buffy assured him. "Could I just take a peek?"

"Unless you already *are* involved . . ." Mr. Flutie insinuated, and Buffy shook her head.

"Never mind."

"Buffy," the principal went on, relenting a little, "I understand this is confusing. You're probably feeling a lot right now. You should share those feelings. With someone else."

Giving him a wan smile, Buffy nodded and backed away.

She had no intention of giving up so easily.

Rushing from the building, she went quickly around the side of the gym. It was easy locating another door to the locker room. She twisted the knob, but the door was locked tight.

Buffy looked around to make certain she was alone. With one quick tug, she pulled the door open, splintering the lock in the process. Then she gave one last glance over her shoulder and slipped inside.

She saw the body at once, lying on the floor stretched out beneath a blanket. Hesitantly she approached it, feeling certain she wasn't going to be at all pleased with what she found. Slowly she folded the blanket down from the corpse's head and shoulders.

Grim frustration flooded Buffy's face. She stared down at the body, nearly seething.

"Oh, *great!*" she exploded.

There on the boy's neck were two distinct bite marks.

Moments later, an exasperated Buffy strode back into the library.

"Okay, what's the sitch?" she demanded.

Giles was standing on the second level, completely engrossed in a book. He looked down as she started up toward him.

"Sorry?" he asked.

"You heard about the dead guy, right?" Buffy retorted. "The dead guy in the locker?"

"Yes."

"Well, it's the weirdest thing. He's got two little holes in his neck, and all his blood's been drained. Isn't that bizarre? Aren't you just going, 'Ooooh . . .' "

Giles let out a sigh. "I was afraid of this."

"Well, I wasn't! It's my first day. I was afraid that I'd be behind in all the classes, that I wouldn't make any friends, that I'd have last month's hair. I didn't think there would be vampires on campus. And I *don't care.*"

"Then why are you here?"

That stopped her, but only for a moment.

"To tell you that I don't care," Buffy stammered. "Which I don't, and . . . have now told you. So, 'bye."

She retreated and started for the door, feeling a little let down by her undignified exit.

"Will he rise again?" Giles asked.

Buffy stopped in midstride. "Who?"

"The boy."

"No, he's just dead."

"Can you be sure?"

Buffy shook her head. "To make you a vampire they have to suck *your* blood and then you have to suck *their* blood. It's a whole big sucking thing. Mostly they'll just take all your blood and then you just die—why am I still talking to you?"

"You have no idea what's going on, do you?" Giles challenged her, his words tightly controlled. "Do you think it's a coincidence, your coming here? That boy was just the beginning."

Buffy turned back and looked up at him. "Oh, why can't you leave me alone?"

"Because you are the Slayer."

She froze. All the clever things she'd been ready to say to him stuck in her throat. She watched as Giles came down the stairs, his gaze very solemn.

"Into every generation, a Slayer is born," Giles intoned. "One girl, in all the world, a Chosen One. One born with the—"

Buffy joined him then, the two of them speaking

together. "—the strength and skill to hunt the vampires—"

Until Giles broke off, letting Buffy finish the words alone. "To stop the spread of their evil blah blah, I've *heard* it, okay?" Buffy threw at him.

Giles looked troubled. "I don't understand this attitude. You've accepted your duty, you've slain vampires before—"

"Well, I have both been there and done that. And I am moving on."

Giles considered this a moment, then asked, "What do you know about this town?"

"It's two hours on the freeway from Neiman Marcus."

Motioning her to wait for him, Giles disappeared into a back room and continued to talk.

"Dig a bit into the history of this place and you'll find there've been a steady stream of fairly odd occurrences. I believe this area is a center of mystical energy. Things gravitate toward it that you might not find elsewhere."

He reappeared with a stack of books.

"Like vampires," Buffy concluded.

She tried to move past him, but he pulled a book from the pile and handed it to her. It resembled the vampire book he had shown her earlier, and while Buffy stared down at it, he continued to heap more books into her arms.

"Like werewolves," Giles went on quickly. "Zombies. Succubi, incubi . . ." He leaned close into her face. "Everything you ever dreaded under your bed and told yourself couldn't be by the light of day."

"What, did you send away for the *Time Life* series?"

Giles actually looked a bit sheepish. "Uh, yes."

"Did you get the free phone?"

"The calendar."

"Cool." Then, remembering her agenda, Buffy stated, "Okay, first of all, I'm a vampire slayer," transferring the books back into his arms. "And second, I'm retired. Hey, I know! Why don't *you* kill them?"

Giles's smile seemed rather surprised. "I'm a Watcher. I haven't the skill."

"Oh, come on. Stake through the heart, a little sunlight—it's like falling off a log."

"The Slayer slays," Giles explained patiently. "The Watcher—"

"Watches?"

"Yes. No!" Giles recovered himself. "He—he—trains her, he prepares her—"

"Prepares me for what?" Buffy was really angry now. "For getting kicked out of school? Losing all my friends? Having to spend all my time fighting for my life and never getting to tell anyone, because it might 'endanger' them? Go ahead." Her gaze was challenging. "Prepare me."

She turned on her heel and left. Giles went out after her.

Both of them had been so intent on their discussion that neither had noticed the shadowy figure lurking in the stacks. But now Xander emerged slowly into the light, a mixture of amusement, excitement, and total disbelief upon his face. He looked down at the copy of *Theories in Trig* that he held in his hands, and then he looked back at the library door. For a long time his lips moved without a sound. And then at last his voice echoed out into the silence.

"What?"

Giles continued to follow Buffy through the hallway as it began filling with students once again.

"It's getting worse," Giles called after her.

Buffy stopped and whirled to face him. All too conscious of the crowds around them, she tried not to sigh too loudly. "What's getting worse?"

"The influx of the undead," Giles murmured, moving her over against the wall. "The supernatural occurrences. It's been building for years, and now . . . there's a reason why you're here, and there's a reason why it's now."

"Because *now* is the time my mom moved *here."*

She started to walk away from him, but he put up one arm to stop her.

"Something is coming," he insisted. "Something is going to happen here soon."

Buffy pulled his arm down. "Gee, can you vague that up for me . . . ?"

But Giles's voice had dropped even more. Buffy had to strain to hear.

"As far as I can tell," he explained, "the signs point to a crucial mystical upheaval very soon—days, possibly less."

Buffy gave him a narrow stare. "Come on. This is Sunnydale," she reminded him. "How bad an evil can there be here?"

Chapter 5

Night had fallen.

And yet it was always night in this dark and evil place, this secret, hidden place where even the flickering candlelight could not quite penetrate the heavy blackness. Shadows slid across damp, crumbling walls, oozing into corners and crevices, slithering silently over the blank, staring faces of broken statuary.

And the human figures, too, resembled statues—strange, soulless reminders of death and decay—as they knelt upon the ground, their faces bent in supplication.

An ominous chanting rose and fell around them . . . rose and fell . . . echoing on and on through the chamber.

Luke kept himself apart from the others. Apart and well ahead of the rest, an imposing figure even upon his knees, his eyes and senses keenly alert. He was large and powerfully built, with wide nostrils and narrowly angled reptilian eyes, thick lips, and a jutting brow. To an innocent onlooker, he might have passed for a young man in his twenties—yet the truth was, Luke was much, much older than that. His clothes reflected long-ago and long-forgotten eras, but spoke definitively of none.

The chanting became louder now . . . more intense. Luke gazed for a long while into the calm, thick surface of a dark red pool. A pool of blood.

"The sleeper will awaken," Luke pronounced.

His voice was deep and resonant; his face was a vampire's face. His breath smelled of graveyards and rotting corpses.

"The sleeper will awaken," Luke said again. "And the world will bleed."

Slowly he dipped his finger in the blood.

"Amen."

And as the candles guttered wildly, the dismal ruins around him were illuminated, but only for one brief instant—the ruins of a church long buried beneath the earth. Stanchions and arches leaned at broken angles, sheeted rock pushed in from all sides. The shiny pool of blood spread itself thickly over what once had been an altar.

The chanting swelled in volume.

It filled the chamber with devotion and despair, trembling every shadow, every heartbeat.

And the faithful waited.

Chapter 6

Buffy stood in front of her bedroom mirror, agonizing over her fashion statement of the evening. Holding up an outfit that was shockingly scanty, she spoke aloud to her reflection.

"Hi! I'm an enormous slut!"

Somehow it wasn't quite right. She replaced it with the second outfit, this one a much plainer version, and took another careful look at herself.

"Hi! Would you like a copy of the *Watchtower?*"

Still not right. Frustrated, she threw them both down.

"I used to be so good at this," she grumbled as her mother came into the room.

"Are you going out tonight, honey?" Joyce asked her.

"Yeah, Mom. I'm going to a club."

"Will there be boys there?"

"No, Mom, it's a nun club."

Her mother ignored the mild sarcasm. "Well, just be careful."

"I will."

Buffy could sense the conversation easing into serious territory. Both she and her mother regarded each other a little uncomfortably.

"I think we can make it work here," Joyce insisted. "I've got my positive energy flowing. I'm gonna get the gallery on its feet—we may already have found a space."

Buffy tried to sound enthusiastic. "Great."

"And that school is a very nurturing environment, which is what you need."

"Mom . . ."

"Oh, not too nurturing. I know. You're sixteen; I read all about the dangers of overnurturing." Joyce hesitated, then added truthfully, "It's hard. New town and all. For me, too. I'm trying to make it work. I'm *going* to make it work."

"I know."

"You're a good girl, Buffy. You just fell in with the wrong crowd. But that's all behind us now."

"It is," Buffy reassured her. "From now on, I'm only hanging out with the living. I—I mean, the lively . . . people."

Her mother looked relieved. "Okay. You have fun."

* * *

She decided on the tight slacks, the powder blue shirt, and the knit tank top to go under it. She decided to put her hair up on top of her head.

And then she decided to walk to the Bronze.

As Buffy left the safe lights of the suburbs behind, she soon found herself entering the deserted city streets on the edge of town.

She turned a corner, wondering how much further she'd have to go. The sidewalk stretched endlessly before her, camouflaged in shadows, and her footsteps echoed hollowly in the dark. She couldn't get that day's events out of her mind, all the people she'd met, all the strange things that had happened. Lost in thought, she continued along the pavement until slowly it began to dawn on her that she wasn't alone.

There was another sound of footsteps now.

Footsteps behind her . . . footsteps walking where she had walked . . .

Buffy whirled around.

She could see a figure standing there, shrouded in blackness. Just far enough away so that she didn't feel quite comfortable confronting it.

The figure didn't move.

And though she couldn't actually see its face, she had the distinct, unsettling impression that it was looking straight at her.

Turning quickly, Buffy went on.

The figure followed.

Buffy picked up speed. She could hear the footsteps again, sure and measured behind her, taking their time. With a twinge of fear, she turned the next corner and went even faster.

The figure kept coming. Not hurrying at all . . . keeping a discreet distance.

On impulse, Buffy ducked into an alleyway, quickly assessing her surroundings. A large pipe spanned the enclosure some ten feet above her. A cluster of smelly garbage cans blocked the other end.

With one smooth movement, Buffy swung herself up onto the pipe, her body poised in a handstand. She waited for the figure to turn into the alleyway, and then she dropped down on him without warning, her legs locked over his neck. Throwing herself back, she tipped him over, then rolled and slammed his body onto the ground.

He was on his feet instantly, but she grabbed him and threw him up against the wall. As she closed in, she suddenly realized he was making no move to attack her. Instead he put up his hands.

"Is there a problem, ma'am?" the young man asked.

He seemed faintly amused at the situation. Buffy eyed him suspiciously, getting a good look at him for the first time.

He was strikingly handsome. Tall and dark, with prominent cheekbones and thick hair, and an unmistakable aloofness in his deep-set eyes. Yet there was something else there, too—glowing far back beyond his gaze—a strange sort of knowing that made Buffy feel slightly uncomfortable. He'd moved swiftly and easily during their scuffle—with a fighter's grace, she'd noted—but now he simply stood there looking back at her.

"There's a problem," Buffy shot back. "Why are you following me?"

His voice was calm. Matter of fact. "I know what you're thinking, but don't worry. I don't bite."

It wasn't at all what she'd expected to hear. She took a step back from him, her face perplexed.

"Truth is, I thought you'd be taller," the young man went on. "Or bigger: muscles and all that. You're pretty spry, though."

"What do you want?" Buffy demanded.

"Same thing you do."

"Okay, what do I want?"

The amusement left his face.

"To kill 'em. To kill 'em all."

Buffy felt a split second of surprise. "Sorry!" She announced, recovering herself neatly, doing her best impression of a game-show host. "That's incorrect, but you do get this lovely watch and a year's supply of Turtle Wax . . . what I *want* . . . is to be left alone."

He gazed at her steadily. "You really think that's an option anymore? You're standing at the mouth of hell. And it's about to open."

Slowly he reached into his coat. When he withdrew his hand again, he was holding what appeared to be a small sort of jewelry box.

"Don't turn your back on this," he warned, throwing it to her. "You've got to be ready."

Buffy's chin lifted defiantly. "What for?"

"For the Harvest."

He turned from her then and started back the way he'd come. Buffy called out after him.

"Who are you?"

"Let's just say I'm a friend," he said quietly.

"Well, maybe I don't want a friend," Buffy answered, exasperated.

His smile was strangely secretive. "I didn't say I was *yours* . . ."

Buffy watched him go. She saw his shadow fading into all the other shadows, and then she carefully opened the box.

It was a cross.

Small and most definitely an antique. Attached to a long silver chain.

She glanced up quickly. The mysterious young man had disappeared.

Chapter 7

A good-sized crowd milled aimlessly around the Bronze.

It certainly wasn't a fancy place, Buffy saw at once—in fact, it was kind of a dive—but there was an appealing sort of earthiness about it that seemed to go with the high-school-and-older crowd standing in line. No standards of coolness here either, she noted—just a simple matter of paying four bucks and getting your hand stamped if you were old enough to drink.

She moved her way up the line, scanning about for a familiar face. There was no one here she recognized. Inside, the place was dark and noisy and absolutely packed. A band blasted wildly from the stage up front, yet the crowds seemed relatively well behaved. A lot of kids were squeezed into the coffee bar at the back, while even more watched the action from the balcony above, lounging at tables set for two.

Buffy pushed her way through, still looking around for someone she knew. A good-looking guy caught her attention and waved, smiling.

Buffy smiled and waved back, then suddenly realized the guy was waving to someone behind her. Embarrassed, she lowered her hand to her head, trying to pretend she'd been fixing her hair. She was relieved when she finally spotted Willow at the bar. The girl was shyly ordering a soda, and Buffy hurried over to join her.

"Hi!" Buffy smiled.

"Oh, hi!" Willow looked surprised and pleased at the same time. And very out of place in her Peter Pan collar and sweater. "Hi."

"Are you here with someone?"

"No, I'm just here. I thought Xander was gonna show up . . ."

"Oh, are you guys going out?"

"No. We're just friends." Willow thought a moment, then added, "We used to go out, but we broke up."

"How come?"

"He stole my Barbie." As Buffy gave her a strange look, Willow explained, "We were five."

"Oh."

"I don't actually date a whole lot . . . lately."

"Why not?"

"Well, when I'm with a boy I like, it's hard for me to say anything cool or witty, or at all . . . I can usually make a few vowel sounds, and then I have to go away."

Buffy couldn't help laughing. "It's not that bad."

"It is. I think boys are more interested in a girl who can talk."

"You really *haven't* been dating lately."

"It's probably easy for you."

"Oh, yeah," Buffy nodded a little forlornly. "Real easy."

"I mean, you don't seem too shy."

"Well, my philosophy is—" Buffy broke off. "Do you wanna hear my philosophy?"

"I do," Willow said eagerly.

"Life is short."

Willow fixed her with a steady gaze. "Life is short."

"Not original, I'll grant you," Buffy shrugged. "But it's true. Why waste time being all shy? Why worry about some guy and if he's gonna laugh at you? You know? Seize the moment. 'Cause tomorrow you might be dead."

"Oh . . ." Willow smiled. "That's nice . . ."

Buffy's glance went quickly around the crowds. As she spotted someone moving about on the balcony above them, her brow creased in a frown.

"Uh, I'll be back in a minute," she promised.

"That's okay," Willow assured her. "You don't have to come back."

Smiling at her friend's self-effacing attitude, Buffy said again, more firmly this time, "I'll be back in a minute."

She wasn't sure if Willow heard. The girl's head was lowered and she was murmuring to herself, "Seize the moment . . ." while Buffy took off again through the crowds.

It didn't take her long to find the stairs. She pushed her way up and onto the balcony, then managed at last to squeeze next to the railing that overlooked the stage. She leaned there trying to appear casual, not even looking at Giles, who came to stand just as casually beside her.

"So, you like to party with the students?" Buffy teased him. "Isn't that kind of skanky?"

Giles's tone was withering. "Right. This is me having fun." He continued to gaze down upon the stage. "Watching Clown-hair prance about is hardly my idea of a party. I'd much prefer to be home with a cup of Bovril and a good book."

Buffy rolled her eyes. "You need a personality, *stat.*"

"This is a perfect breeding ground for vampire activity," Giles admonished her. "Dark, crowded . . . besides, I knew you were likely to show up. And I have to make you understand—"

"That the Harvest is coming, I know, your friend told me."

Giles seemed completely thrown off by this remark. He shot Buffy an anxious glance. "What did you say?"

"The . . . Harvest," she said carefully. "That means something to you? 'Cause I'm drawing a blank."

"I'm not sure. . . . Who told you this?"

"This guy." She could still see him in her mind, could still recall their confrontation in the alley. "Dark, gorgeous in an annoying sort of way. I figured you were buds."

"No . . ." Giles mumbled, frowning. "The Harvest. . . . Did he say anything else?"

"Something about the mouth of hell. I really didn't like him."

They were both staring out over the floor now at the kids dancing and partying to the loud rhythm of the band.

"Look at them," Giles's tone bordered on annoyance. "Throwing themselves about . . . completely unaware of the danger that surrounds them."

"Lucky them . . ."

"Or perhaps you're right," he conceded. "Perhaps there *is* no trouble coming. The signs could be wrong. It's not as though you're having the nightmares . . ."

At the mention of the word, Buffy's face suddenly clouded. She gazed down at all the happy faces below her and said nothing at all.

Chapter 8

Cordelia stood off to one side at a safe distance from the writhing crowds. She stood there with her usual friends and her usual air of disdain.

"My mom doesn't even get out of bed anymore," she announced, sounding bored. "The doctor says it's Epstein-Barr. I'm, like, '*Please,* it's chronic hepatitis or at *least* chronic fatigue syndrome.' I mean nobody cool has Epstein-Barr anymore."

She stiffened a little as she saw Jesse approaching. He walked right past the others in her group and turned his smile straight on her.

"Cordelia!"

"Oh, yay," Cordelia replied. "It's my stalker."

"Hey, you look great."

"Well, I'm glad we had this chat—" she began, but Jesse cut her off.

"Listen, I, um, do you wanna dance?"

Cordelia's tone was withering. "With you?"

"Well, uh, yeah."

"Well, uh, no."

She took off, her loyal entourage in tow, while Jesse stood there helplessly, alone with his pain.

"Fine," he said, managing at last to muster some dignity. "Plenty of other fish in the sea. Oh, yeah. I'm on the prowl. Witness me prowling."

He looked around at the room full of people, appraised the situation, and officially began his prowl.

Up above on the balcony, Buffy stood watching him disappear into the crowds. She was still shaken by Giles's comments about the nightmares, and she could feel her defenses starting to crumble.

"I didn't say I'd *never* slay another vampire," she tried to rationalize. "I'm just not gonna get way extracurricular with it. If I run into one, sure . . ."

"But will you be ready?" Giles asked earnestly. "There's so much you don't know about them and about your own powers. A vampire appears to be a normal person until the feed is upon him. Only then does he reveal his true demonic visage."

"You're like a textbook with arms!" Buffy exploded. "I know this!"

Giles chose to ignore her outburst. "The point is, a Slayer should be able to see them anyway. Without looking, without thinking. Can you tell me if there's a vampire in this building?"

Buffy hesitated. "Maybe?"

"You should know! Even through this mass and

this din you should be able to sense them." Giles drew a breath, his voice encouraging. "Try. Reach out with your mind."

Buffy looked down at the mass of swinging, swaying bodies. Slowly she furrowed her brow.

"You have to hone your senses," Giles instructed her. "Focus until the energy washes over you, till you can feel every particle of—"

"There's one," Buffy said quickly.

Giles stopped. He peered down over the railing, completely nonplussed. "What? Where?"

Pointing, Buffy tried to show him. "Down there. Talking to that girl."

In one far corner stood a good-looking young man. He was talking to a girl, but from where they were standing, neither Giles nor Buffy could really get a good look at her.

Giles cast Buffy a doubtful look. "But you don't know—" he began, while Buffy vehemently interrupted.

"Oh, please! Look at his jacket. He's got the sleeves rolled up. And the shirt . . . deal with that outfit for a moment."

Again Giles looked perplexed. "It's dated?"

"It's carbon dated! Trust me—only someone who's been living underground for ten years would think that was the look."

"But . . . you didn't *hone* . . ."

Buffy scarcely heard him. She leaned farther out over the balcony and murmured, "Oh, no . . ."

The vampire was still chatting with the girl in the corner. Only now he was motioning her to come with him, and as she finally stepped into view, a sick feeling of dread rose in the pit of Buffy's stomach.

"Isn't that—" Giles began.

"Willow."

"What is she doing?"

"Seizing the moment," Buffy threw back at him as she started for the stairs.

For one brief instant she caught a glimpse of them—the vampire and Willow—moving toward the back door near the stage. She fought her way down the steps and through the mobs across the floor, but when she looked again, Willow had disappeared. Worried, Buffy scanned the room, then headed for the backstage door. She felt as if she were moving in slow motion; the closer she got to the stage, the more crowded it seemed to grow. In frustration, she finally managed to wrestle through the rest of the way and shove open the door.

The shock of the darkness took her by surprise, but only for a second. It was empty backstage, cool and strangely muffled. There was no one about, and Buffy moved slowly, cautiously, along the postered brick walls, ready for anything. She passed an old chair propped in a corner and on impulse, she snapped off one of its legs, holding it close to her like a makeshift stake. After the noise and crush of bodies inside the club, the place seemed vast and mysterious. At last she found the exit door. It opened into an alley, but this, too, was deserted, and with a growing sense of danger Buffy headed back for the main door.

She didn't expect him to be there as she turned the corner.

With lightning speed Buffy grabbed the shadowy figure, threw him up against the wall, then held him there, two feet off the ground.

She stared fiercely into the vampire's face . . .

And realized too late that it wasn't a vampire at all.

Cordelia hung there in her grasp, wearing the same dumbfounded expression that her other friends wore as they trooped out of the bathroom.

"Cordelia!" Buffy stammered, while the girl continued to hang there, gaping at her.

"Excuse me . . . could you be any weirder?" Cordelia burst out. "Is there a more weirdness that you could have?"

Sheepishly, Buffy let the girl down and lowered the stake discreetly to her side.

"God," Cordelia sneered. "What is your childhood trauma?"

Buffy tried to recover herself. She faked a cheerful expression and asked brightly, "Did you guys see Willow? Did she come by here?"

"Why?" Cordelia shot back. "Did you need to attack *her* with a stick?"

With a red face and shaken nerves, Buffy quickly retreated, leaving Cordelia and her entourage still gazing after her in disbelief.

"Excuse me," Cordelia grumbled, pulling her flip phone from her purse. "I have to call everyone I've ever met right now."

Buffy hurried back to the stage door and let herself into the club. She spotted Giles at once, waiting for her at the foot of the stairs, and she went over to join him.

"That was fast." Giles looked relieved. "Well done. I'd best go to the library. This Harvest is—"

"I didn't find them," Buffy said, her frustrated glance going around the room.

Giles stared at her as though he'd misunderstood. "The vampire's not dead?"

"No, but my social life is on the critical list."

"What do we do?"

"You go on. I'll take care of it."

"I should come with you, no?" Giles offered, but Buffy shook her head at him and started off again through the crowds.

"Don't worry," she said. "One vampire I can handle."

She didn't really see Jesse as she brushed past him. She had her mind on other, more important things, and Jesse was too busy talking to a girl even to notice that Buffy had gone by.

"What did you say your name was?" Jesse asked again, hoping this time his luck might change.

She didn't look familiar to him. Definitely not from class . . . not even from campus. Though of course, he had no way of knowing that she'd broken into the school last night. That she'd been on a date with a certain young man . . . the same young man found dead just this afternoon, stuffed inside a locker . . .

"Darla," the girl answered, smiling at him.

She had a really cute face, and Jesse smiled back.

"Darla. I haven't seen you before. Are you from around here?"

"No, but I've got family here."

"Have I met them?"

Darla's smile widened. Her teeth were pretty and white. "You probably will," she promised.

Chapter 9

Cloistered within the moldering walls of their sanctuary, the disciples continued their ritual.

It was a ritual as ancient as evil itself, and slowly, slowly, the impassioned voices rose as one. Soon the ceremony would reach its long-awaited climax. And where this church had once resonated with the heartfelt vows of the virtuous, the only sounds that filled it now were these mocking prayers of the damned.

Beside the altar Luke suddenly looked up.

He stared for a moment, eyes wide with religious fervor, and then he began to back away. As though in obedience to his signal, the others also began moving back, their voices quivering with expectancy.

Still, Luke prayed above the pool. Without warning, a head thrust up from the bloody depths, and

Luke started, staring in wonder, taking yet another step away.

The head continued to rise, and with it the tall, elegant figure of a king long sleeping, his massive body gleaming with dark, rich blood.

The Master was the most powerful of all the vampires. Born Heinrich Joseph Nest some six hundred years ago, he was dressed completely in black, both frightening and awesome to behold. His face did not resemble anything human; he was as much demon as man. His regal bearing spoke of invincibility—commanded reverence, submission, and undying loyalty. As he stepped forward, extending one hand, Luke grasped it with humble and utter devotion.

"Master . . ." Luke mumbled.

Again the Master moved forward, his face still cloaked in half darkness. Luke withdrew several respectful paces and the Master looked about for a moment as though considering.

"Luke."

"Master . . ."

"I am weak."

"Come the Harvest, you'll be restored," Luke promised.

"The Harvest . . ."

"We're almost there. Soon you'll be free."

The Master walked past Luke. Once more he reached out his hand, but this time, as he did so, the air before him began to ripple slightly, forming a sort of mystical wall that enclosed him.

Abruptly he pulled back his hand.

"I must be ready," the Master said. "I need my strength."

"I've sent your servants to bring you some food," Luke reassured him.

"Good." Then, as Luke started out, "Luke . . ."

Luke stopped at once. "Yes?"

"Bring me something . . . young."

Chapter 10

Willow was definitely having second thoughts.

As she and her date walked along through the dark, she could feel herself growing increasingly nervous. He hadn't said half a dozen words since they'd left the Bronze, and there was just something different about him that hadn't been so obvious back there in all the noise and bright lights. *And all the people,* she thought to herself.

"Sure is dark." She made a feeble attempt at conversation, but it didn't make her feel any braver.

"It's night," her date replied.

"That's a dark time." Willow nodded. "Night. Traditionally."

They walked farther. Again she tried to start a conversation.

"I still can't believe I've never seen you at school. Do you have Mr. Chomsky for History?"

The boy didn't answer. He just suddenly stopped.

Willow glanced around uneasily. "The ice-cream bar's down this way," she directed him. "It's past Hamilton Street."

She watched as his hand reached out, as it firmly took hold of hers.

"I know a shortcut," he said.

And then he led her toward the cemetery . . . into the darkness of the woods.

Buffy couldn't find Willow anywhere.

With growing anxiety, she hurried around from the back of the club and saw Xander coming down the sidewalk, his skateboard tucked under one arm.

"You're leaving already?" Xander asked, but Buffy wasn't in the mood for chatting.

"Xander, have you seen Willow?"

"Not tonight."

"I need to find her. She left with a guy."

"We are talking about Willow, right?" Xander sounded impressed. "Scoring at the Bronze. Work it, girlfriend."

Buffy was oblivious to his humor. "Where would they go?"

"Why, you know something about Mr. Goodbar that she doesn't?" Xander pretended to have a sudden brainstorm and rubbed his hands together. "Oh! Hey. I hope he's not a *vampire.* 'Cause then you'd have to *slay* him."

This time he got her full attention. With a look of

surprise—and undisguised annoyance—she turned back to stare at him.

"Was there a school bulletin? Was it in the news? Is there anybody in this town who *doesn't* know I'm a Slayer?"

"I only know that you *think* you're a Slayer. And I only know that 'cause I was in the library today."

"Whatever." Buffy was painfully aware of the passing of time. "Just tell me where Willow would go."

"You're serious."

"We don't find her, there's gonna be another dead body in the morning."

Xander hesitated, studying her solemn expression. It dawned on him then that she wasn't kidding. That she was, in fact, very dead serious.

"Come on," he said.

Willow had passed the point of nervousness.

As she and her date continued on through the woods, she realized she was easing into quiet panic. Her mind spun helplessly as she tried to figure out how she'd managed to get herself into such a scary situation—and how on earth she was going to get herself out again.

"Okay," she said at last. "This is nice and . . . scary. . . . Are you sure this is faster?"

Still her date said nothing. She couldn't be certain, of course, but every instinct warned her that this probably *wasn't* the way to the ice-cream bar.

And then, as he suddenly stopped, she realized they were standing outside a small mausoleum.

Confused, Willow stared at the crumbling entrance. A well of thick blackness yawned before her, and a cold chill crept up her spine.

"Hey," her date spoke at last. "You ever been in one of these?"

Willow tried to keep her voice from shaking, tried to sound assertive. "No, thank you."

But he was moving in on her now, pulling her hair back from her neck. Holding her intimately . . . holding her much closer than she wanted to be held . . .

"Come on," he tempted her, his voice teasing. "What are you afraid of?"

And then he pushed her through the doorway.

Willow stumbled in, terrified. She couldn't see a thing and she blinked rapidly, trying to adjust her eyes to the dark. After several agonizing seconds, she was able to make out a small room with carved stone walls. A huge tomb took up most of the center, with a stone figure of a man lying on top of it. Behind her was the door she'd come in; ahead of her was a much smaller iron door that was locked shut.

Willow spun around. She could see her date now, his silhouette filling the entrance to the mausoleum, blocking her escape. Her heart thudded frantically in her ears.

"That wasn't funny." She tried to sound calm and in control, but her voice was dangerously close to tears.

The boy didn't respond. Instead he stepped closer, his face bathed in shadows. Willow circled away from him, trying to get closer to the door.

"I think I'm gonna go," she told him.

"Is *that* what you think?"

There was no playfulness in his voice. Willow heard the danger there and instinctively took a step back, and then another. And then she turned and squealed as she ran straight into Darla.

Darla seemed to be appraising the situation. She looked first at Willow and then at Willow's date.

"Is this the best you could do?" Darla asked him.

The boy's voice sounded slightly defensive. "She's fresh."

"Hardly enough to share," Darla returned, walking casually down the steps and across the floor. "Why didn't you bring your own?"

"I did."

Darla indicated the doorway just behind her. As Willow watched in fearful confusion, a very dazed Jesse stumbled in.

"Hey, wait up," Jesse called to Darla.

"Jesse!" Willow hurried over to him, relieved. He was clutching his neck and looked slightly feverish. In truth, he didn't seem particularly aware that Willow was even there.

"I think you gave me a hickey." Again he spoke to Darla, who pointedly ignored him.

Willow watched as Jesse took his hand from his neck. She could see blood on his fingers, blood on his throat. She gazed at him for a moment in disbelief, then looked at the other two figures behind her, her eyes going wide.

"I got hungry on the way," Darla shrugged.

Willow took hold of Jesse, pulling desperately on his arms. "Jesse, let's get out of here."

"You're not going anywhere," Darla informed her.

"Leave us alone," Willow tried to sound forceful, but Darla advanced on her so swiftly that she didn't even have time to back away.

"You're not going anywhere," Darla muttered, "until we've *fed!*"

As she spat out the last word, she thrust her face right into Willow's. And before Willow's horrified eyes, Darla's face began to change—to shift and slither into something grotesque—rotting skin, teeth gleaming razor sharp, a grin that was as ravenous as it was evil—

Willow screamed. She stumbled backward and fell. Through a haze of terror she could see her date laughing now, circling her slowly, his predator's face every bit as hideous and repulsive as the girl's had become.

Willow knew she was going to die. She watched as the creatures closed in on her, knifelike fingernails reaching out, mouths drooling, eyes glistening hungrily. When the voice suddenly spoke out behind them, she thought at first that it wasn't—couldn't *possibly* be—real.

"Well, this is nice," the voice said pleasantly.

Buffy stepped into the room with Xander following.

Everybody froze.

"A little bare," Buffy observed, running one hand across the dusty tomb, "but a dash of paint, a few throw pillows—call it home."

"Who the hell are you?" Darla growled.

"Wow, you mean there's actually somebody around here who doesn't know already?" Buffy tossed back. "That's a relief. I'm telling you, having a secret identity in this town is a job of work."

As Buffy held their attention, Xander moved in between the two vampires. Nothing had quite prepared the creatures for this unexpected turn of events, and they slowly loosened their grips on Willow and Jesse.

"Buffy, we bail now, right?" Xander prompted, but Willow's date had managed to recover himself a little.

"Not yet," he snarled.

"Okay, first of all, what's with this outfit?" Buffy baited him. "Live in the now, okay? You look like DeBarge." Then turning to Darla, she added, completely unperturbed, "Now, we can do this the hard way, or . . . well, actually, there's just the hard way."

Darla stood her ground. "Fine with me."

"You sure?" Buffy persisted. "It's not gonna be pretty. We're talking violence, strong language, adult content."

Even as she spoke, Willow's date rushed her from behind, charging with lightning speed. With one graceful motion, Buffy whipped a stake out from beneath her jacket and stuck it out behind her. There was a dull puncture sound as the creature impaled himself. He stopped, eyes round with surprise, and then he thudded to the floor.

Buffy never even looked at him.

As he hit the ground, his body crumbled to dust.

"See what happens when you roughhouse?" Buffy told Darla.

Xander and Willow were speechless. All they could do was stare at the cold, empty floor where a body had lain only seconds ago. Darla, on the other hand, was wide-eyed and wary, but definitely not cowed. She moved slowly around Buffy, preparing to fight the girl herself.

"He was young," Darla said in disgust. "And stupid."

"Xander, go," Buffy ordered.

"Don't go far," Darla echoed.

Without warning she lunged at Buffy. Buffy met her head-on, parrying Darla's blows with martial arts precision, while Xander herded the others out.

The three ran as quickly as they could through the woods, Willow and Xander half dragging, half carrying Jesse. No one spoke. They were all still trying to cope with the reality of what they'd just seen back there in the mausoleum. *Buffy . . . the Slayer . . .*

As Buffy got in another effective blow, Darla hit the ground painfully. Buffy wasn't joking anymore. She was sweaty and breathless, and all the humor had drained from her face.

"You know, I just wanted to start over," she said peevishly, planting one foot on Darla's chest. "Be like everybody else. Have some friends, maybe a dog . . . but no. You had to come here. You couldn't go suck on some other town."

"Who *are* you?" Darla glared up at her, fury in her eyes.

"Don't you know?"

But before Buffy could go on, a pair of hands suddenly grabbed her by the throat and lifted her bodily from the ground.

"I don't care," Luke said slowly.

She hadn't sensed him behind her. As Luke stepped from the shadows, his enormous bulk made her seem tiny and insignificant, and Buffy realized the odds were now dangerously against her. Luke tossed her into the air with no effort at all, hurling her a good fifteen feet. She landed badly and hit the wall with her face.

Luke turned on Darla, who was struggling to get up.

"You were supposed to be bringing an offering for the Master," he berated her. "We're almost at Harvest, and you dally with this child?"

"We had someone." Frightened now, Darla tried to defend herself. "But *she* came and . . . she killed Thomas . . . Luke, she's strong."

Luke fixed her with a contemptuous stare. "You go. I'll see if I can handle the little girl."

Buffy was trying to lift herself off the floor when Luke closed in and grabbed her. He'd counted on her being stunned, but she was ready for him this time. She knocked his arms away, then kicked him smartly in the face. It sent him back just a little, but he recovered himself almost instantly, landing a solid punch to her jaw.

"You *are* strong," Luke muttered. He slammed her back to the ground and gave a throaty laugh. "I'm stronger."

But Buffy had no intention of giving up. Wrestling away from him at last, she got to her feet and circled slowly around the tomb, keeping it safely between her and Luke.

"You're wasting my time," Luke said calmly.

"Hey," Buffy retorted, "I had other plans, too, okay?"

Luke shoved at the lid of the tomb. As the heavy stone slab flew straight at her, Buffy leaped over it and jumped on top. With one swift movement, she flipped over and planted both feet solidly on Luke's chest. The momentum caused both of them to fall, but Buffy managed to get up first, pulling out her stake and driving it toward his chest. Luke's hand shot out and grabbed it just before it made contact.

"You think you can stop me?" Luke's face was twisted with rage. "Stop us?"

He squeezed his fist. The stake splintered like a matchstick in his powerful grip and he punched Buffy violently, knocking her backward.

"You have no idea what you're dealing with," he snarled.

Victorious now, he stood over her. His voice lowered, and he began to intone the sacred text.

"And like a plague of boils, the race of man

covered the earth. But on the third day of the newest light will come the Harvest . . ."

Buffy hovered on the very edge of consciousness. Her head spun in slow motion, distorted thoughts flashing in and out of her muddled brain.

She seemed to see Giles standing back in his library, poring over his ancient books with growing consternation. He was staring down at one page in particular—an old engraving which depicted a cruel and vicious massacre . . .

". . . When the blood of men will flow as wine . . ." Luke went on.

The people in the engraving writhed about in their own blood, and in the very center of them all stood a creature bearing a three-pointed star upon his forehead, feeding off a woman . . .

". . . When the Master will walk among them once more . . ."

As Luke's voice droned steadily on, the images suddenly shifted. Now Buffy could see the crumbling ruins of an old church; she could sense an awesome danger emanating from a figure bathed in darkness.

". . . The world will belong to the Old Ones . . ." Luke recited.

Willow, Xander and Jesse hurried through the forest.

"We'll get the police," Willow gasped. "It's just a few blocks up—"

Willow's voice broke off. The three of them

stopped and stared, expressions of utter despair creeping over their faces.

Three vampires stood waiting for them. Even as the three friends backed off . . . even as they suddenly realized that Darla was right behind them . . .

Buffy forced her eyes open. She got unsteadily to her feet, all the while keeping her wary gaze on Luke.

". . . and hell itself will come to town." Luke finished at last.

Buffy tried to move sideways, to get away from him—but he struck her with savage force. Helplessly she flew backward and landed inside the tomb. She landed hard upon her back, all the wind knocked out of her. She turned her head slowly to the side and saw the withered, decaying corpse of the tomb's owner.

She could tell she was badly hurt. She couldn't see Luke anymore, couldn't see anything but the damp, moldy walls of the tomb, though she strained her eyes desperately through the darkness. *He could be anywhere,* she realized. *Anywhere* . . .

Slowly, achingly, she lifted her head. She was really frightened now—more frightened than she'd ever been in her life. Very cautiously she peered over one side of the tomb.

Nothing.

Only silence.

With her heart wildly hammering, Buffy tried to look over the opposite edge.

Luke jumped out of nowhere, roaring triumphantly, filling her vision, filling the room, throwing himself into the crypt on top of her.

She tried frantically to fight him off, but he pinned her with no effort at all. And then he simply stared down at her, contemplating her with gleeful animal hunger.

His teeth dripped a thick string of spittle. She could feel it sliding over her cheek.

"Amen," Luke grinned.

And then he bore down on her.

Chapter 11

Through a haze of terror Buffy could see Luke's monstrous face, his lips curled back from his gums, his fangs bared greedily, moving closer and closer to her neck. She twisted and fought with all her strength, but her struggles were useless against him.

With one quick slash of his fingernails, Luke pulled her shirt open, just wide enough to expose her throat. Buffy gasped, bracing herself for the quick, searing stab of his teeth—but instead, Luke let out a shriek and jumped back.

Buffy stared at him, her mind reeling in confusion. Smoke was streaming from his hand, and he was glaring at his palm, eyes blazing with fury and shock.

As Buffy's own gaze lowered to her chest, she saw a silver cross lying there—the cross that the mysterious guy had given her earlier that night. Somehow it had slipped free from her inside pocket and come in contact with Luke's hand during the struggle.

Buffy wasted no time. With a burst of renewed energy, she kicked at Luke with both legs, sending him flying from the tomb. Before he could recover, she leaped out and ran for the door.

The beating had taken a toll on her—much more than she'd realized, Buffy thought glumly. Now as she tried to run through the woods, she was all too aware of the lightness in her head, the rubbery feeling in her legs, the painful heaving of her chest. She stumbled through the graveyard as fast as she could. When she finally reached the opposite edge of the trees, she stopped and looked behind her in the direction of the mausoleum.

She was alone.

Nobody seemed to be following her . . . not even the shadows were moving.

And then she heard Willow scream. "No! Nooo! Get—off—"

Adrenaline pumping, Buffy raced toward the sound of her friend's voice. As she burst upon the scene, she could see Willow on the ground, wrestling with a vampire. The creature held Willow mercilessly in his grasp. He was just going in for her neck when Buffy surprised him, causing him to look up.

It was just the chance Buffy needed.

With one swift kick to his face, she sent the vampire sprawling backward. He gave a grunt of pain, then staggered to his feet, holding his nose and trying to get away from her.

Buffy stood there a second, catching her breath. All her senses were at their most alert now, and she furiously scanned her surroundings. She heard a cracking sound followed by unmistakable scuffling, and again she took off, leaving Willow still sitting there on the ground, her eyes huge with fright, her body trembling. She sat awhile longer, pulling herself together, then at last she got up and followed the path Buffy had taken.

It didn't take Buffy long to find what she was looking for. Almost immediately she caught sight of Xander, his unconscious body being dragged away by two more vampires. As they sensed an unwelcome presence behind them, the vampires slowly turned around.

It wasn't Buffy they saw, suddenly appearing through the trees. It was Willow. As Willow realized that Xander was in mortal danger, she seemed to change right before their eyes, her expression fiercely threatening.

The vampires turned back again, but Buffy stood there blocking their escape. It was easy to take them both out. With one quick punch, Buffy knocked them off their feet and they scrambled to get up and get away.

But they didn't scramble fast enough.

Grabbing a branch from a nearby tree, Buffy snapped it off and held it in her hand like a stake. She charged one vampire, nailing him neatly through the chest, while the other fled for his life.

Willow ran up to Xander and knelt beside him,

cradling his head in her arms. To her relief he seemed to be coming to, and after blinking a few times, he frowned up at her, trying to get his bearings.

"Xander . . . are you okay?" Willow asked softly.

"Man . . ." Xander still seemed a little disoriented. "Something hit me . . ."

Buffy walked a few paces, peering hard through the trees, her expression solemn and worried. "Where's Jesse?"

For the first time Willow seemed to realize that Jesse was missing. "I don't know," she shook her head. "They surrounded us—he was really weak . . ."

"That girl grabbed him," Xander mumbled. "Took off."

"Which way?" Buffy demanded, but Xander looked blank.

"I don't know."

Buffy stared into the night. She honed all her senses, reaching out, straining through the darkness—but there was nothing . . .

Nothing at all.

Buffy's heart felt heavy and sad.

"Jesse . . ." she whispered.

CHAPTER 12

Things certainly didn't look any brighter the next morning.

Even in the peaceful calm of the school library, a feeling of doom hung thick in the air. No one had gotten any sleep, and Jesse was still missing. Buffy couldn't remember when she'd been so sore; her body ached all over and her brain felt numb. She'd had to hide her injuries from her mother, so now she rummaged through Giles's office for some makeshift bandages. Giles stood at the railing on the upper level of bookshelves and tried to give Xander and Willow an explanation for what was happening.

"This world is older than any of you know," he told them solemnly, spinning a globe for emphasis. "And contrary to popular mythology, it did not begin as a paradise. For untold eons, demons walked the earth. Made it their home . . . their hell."

Willow and Xander both listened intently, their expressions every bit as grave as Giles's own.

"In time they lost their purchase on this reality," he continued, carrying an armload of books down the stairs, "and the way was made for the mortal animals. For man. What remains of the Old Ones are vestiges. Certain magics, certain creatures . . ."

"And vampires," Buffy added.

She emerged at last from Giles's office, wrapping a bandage around her forearm. Xander stood up, clearly agitated.

"Okay, this is where I have a problem, see, because we're now talking about vampires." He frowned. "We're having a talk with vampires in it."

"Isn't that what we saw last night?" Willow asked.

"No, those weren't vampires," Buffy quipped. "Those were just some guys in thundering need of a facial. Or maybe they had rabies—coulda been rabies. And that guy turning to dust . . . just a trick of the light." She ignored the look Xander gave her and regarded him with total understanding. "That's exactly what I said the first time I saw a vampire. I mean, when I was done with the screaming part."

"Oooh . . ." Willow murmured. "I need to sit down."

"You *are* sitting down," Buffy reminded her.

"Oh." Willow gave a vacant nod. "Good for me."

"So vampires are demons?" Xander went on, while Giles again tried to clarify.

"The books tell that the last demon to leave this reality fed off a human, mixed their blood. He was a human form possessed—infected—by the demon's soul." Giles handed Xander one of the heavy volumes. "He bit another, and another . . . and so they walk the earth feeding. Killing some, mixing their blood with others to make more of their kind. Waiting for the animals to die out and the Old Ones to return."

Even as Giles was speaking, two vampires were returning to their lair.

Far below the earth, where the morning sun never reached, Luke and Darla dragged Jesse along the dark, dank tunnel toward the church. Jesse staggered between them, his consciousness slowly returning at last—and as his eyes grew accustomed to the blackness, terror rose sickeningly in his throat.

He looked at the two inhuman faces on either side and then at the mouth of the tunnel they were pulling him through. They seemed to be inside an old pipe, huge and cracked and slimy with mold. As they hauled him the rest of the way, he felt himself being propelled down a pile of rocks and onto a cold, damp floor.

His eyes widened in alarm. A church? It *looked* like a church—or what had once *been* a church—and yet this was a foul, evil place; he could feel it in every fiber of his being.

Jesse looked around, a strange sort of wonder

mixed with his fear. He could see now that he was standing before an altar. An altar and what appeared to be a thick red pool . . .

And then from the total darkness, something moved. Moved and gathered itself from the endless shadows as it slowly emerged and came toward him.

The Master regarded his servants with a cold, imperious stare. He turned his gaze on Jesse, and then at last he spoke.

"Is this for me?"

"An offering, Master," Luke replied humbly.

"He's a good one," Darla added. "His blood is pure."

The Master's voice was quiet. Cunningly innocuous. "You've tasted it."

Realizing her mistake, Darla stepped back in fear. The Master bestowed her a taunting smile.

"I'm your faithful dog. You bring me scraps."

"I didn't mean to—" Darla stammered, but the Master cut her off.

"I have waited. For three-score years I have waited. While you come and go I have been stuck here." His voice rose, trembling with his power. "Here, in a house of *worship*. My ascension is almost at hand."

He broke off. He clutched Darla's face between his fingers.

"Pray that when it comes . . ." he snarled, "I'm in a better mood."

"Master, forgive me," Darla begged him. "We had more offerings, but there was trouble. A girl."

Luke nodded affirmation. "There *was* a girl. She fought well and she knew of our breed. It's possible that she may be . . ."

The Master calmly turned to him. "A Slayer?"

"A Slayer," Giles continued to explain.

"And that would be a what?" Xander asked him.

"As long as there have been vampires, there has been the Slayer," Giles recited. "One girl in all the world—"

"He loves doing this part," Buffy interrupted.

"All right," Giles conceded, speeding up a little. "They hunt vampires, one Slayer dies, the next is called, Buffy is the Slayer, don't tell anyone." He stopped and drew a breath. "I think that's all the vampire information you need."

"Except for one thing," Xander spoke up. "How do you kill them?"

"You don't," Buffy corrected him. "I do."

"Well, Jesse—"

"Jesse's my responsibility. I let him get taken."

Xander frowned. "That's not true."

"If you hadn't shown up," Willow added loyally, "they would have . . . taken us, too. . . . Does anybody mind if I pass out?"

"Breathe . . ." Buffy ordered her.

Willow nodded. "Breathe."

"Breathe," Buffy said again, and then to Giles, "This big guy, Luke, he talked about an offering to the Master. I don't know who or what that was, but if they weren't just feeding, Jesse may still be alive. I'm *gonna* find him."

Calmer now, Willow offered a suggestion. "This is probably a dumb question, but shouldn't we call the police?"

"And they'd believe us, of course," Giles replied.

"We don't have to say vampires," Willow stammered. "We could say there was . . . a bad man."

Buffy shook her head consolingly. "They couldn't handle it if they *did* come. They'd only show up with guns."

"You've no idea where they took Jesse?" Giles asked her.

"I looked around, but . . . soon as they got clear of the woods they could have just—" Buffy made a quick motion with her hand. *"—whoom."*

"Can they *fly?"* Xander looked surprised.

"They can drive."

"Oh."

Willow tried to think back. "I don't remember hearing a car."

"Well, let's take an enormous intuitive leap and say they went underground," Giles said.

"Vampires really jam on sewer systems," Buffy agreed. "You can get anywhere in town without catching any rays. I didn't see any access around there, though."

Xander shrugged. "Well, there's electrical tunnels. They run under the whole town."

For a moment Giles considered this. "If we had a

diagnostic of the tunnel system, it might indicate a meeting place. I suppose we could go to the building commission—"

"We *so* don't have time," Buffy cut him off.

"Uh, guys?" Willow said tentatively. "There may be another way."

CHAPTER 13

"A Slayer . . ." The Master pondered this possibility. "Have you any proof?"

Luke answered him with a sneer. "Only that she fought me and yet lives."

"Very nearly proof enough," the Master conceded. "I can't remember the last time that happened."

"Eighteen forty-three." Luke looked almost embarrassed. "In Madrid. Caught me sleeping."

The Master gave a vague nod. "She mustn't be allowed to interfere with the Harvest."

"I would never let that happen."

"You needn't worry. I believe she'll come to us." As his two servants looked at him questioningly, the Master added, "We have something that she wants. If she *is* a Slayer and this boy lives, she'll try to save him."

Luke walked over to Jesse. His hideous face split in a macabre smile.

"I thought you nothing more than a meal, boy," he chuckled. "Congratulations. You've just been upgraded to 'bait.' "

True to the Master's prediction, Buffy was even at that moment trying to plan a rescue.

"There it is," Buffy said eagerly.

Willow sat at the computer while everyone else gathered around her. Showing on the screen was a complete map of the city's electrical tunnels.

"This runs under the graveyard," Willow explained, pointing to one in particular, but Xander shook his head.

"I don't see any access."

"So all the city plans are just open to the public?" Giles asked.

"Uh, well, in a way," Willow frowned a little sheepishly. "I sort of stumbled onto them when I accidentally . . . decrypted the city council's security system."

Xander's focus remained on the screen. "Someone's been naughty . . ."

"There's nothing here," Buffy sounded disappointed. "This is useless!"

"I think you should ease up on yourself," Giles consoled her, but Buffy turned on him, obviously distressed.

"You're the one who told me I wasn't prepared enough. Understatement. I thought I was on top of it, and then that monster Luke came out of nowhere—"

She broke off abruptly and Xander glanced up at her.

"What?" Xander asked.

But Buffy was remembering the scenes from the past night playing out perfectly in her mind. "He didn't come out of nowhere," she said excitedly. "He came from behind me. I was facing the entrance. He came from behind me and he didn't follow me out." She looked at the other three faces around her. "The access to the tunnels is in the mausoleum."

"Are you sure?" Giles straightened.

"The girl must have doubled back with Jesse after I got out," Buffy went on. "God, I'm so mentally challenged!"

Xander stepped back, ready for action. "So what's the plan? We saddle up, right?"

"There's no 'we,'" Buffy corrected him. "I'm the Slayer and you're not."

"I knew you were gonna throw that in my face," Xander grumbled.

"Xander, this is deeply dangerous."

"I'm inadequate. That's fine. I'm less than a man."

Xander turned his back on her and walked off. With a sympathetic glance in Xander's direction, Willow appealed to Buffy.

"Buffy, I'm not anxious to go into a dark place full of monsters, but I do want to help. I need to."

"Then help me," Giles replied without hesitation. "I've been researching this Harvest affair. Seems to be some sort of preordained massacre. Rivers of blood, hell on earth . . . quite charmless. I am fuzzy on the details, however, and it may be that you can wrest some information from that dread machine."

He paused, glancing from one uncomprehending look to another.

"That was a bit British, wasn't it?" he admitted, embarrassed.

Buffy smiled. "Welcome to the new world."

"I want you to go on the Net," Giles translated.

"Oh!" Willow brightened. "Yeah. Sure. I can do that."

"Then I'm out of here," Buffy announced. "If Jesse's alive, I'll bring him back."

Giles stepped forward, his grave expression softening. "Do I have to tell you to be careful?"

Buffy met his eyes for a long moment.

And then she went out.

She headed across the school grounds toward the outer gate. It was standing wide open, but before she could go through, Mr. Flutie suddenly appeared behind her.

"And where do we think we're going?" Mr. Flutie greeted her.

"We?" Buffy was all innocence. "I? Me?"

Mr. Flutie gave her a patronizing look. "We're not leaving school grounds, are we?"

"No! I'm just . . . admiring the fence. This is quality fencework."

"Because if we *were* leaving school grounds on our second day at a new school after being kicked out of our old school for delinquent behavior—" The principal paused, drawing a breath. "Do you see where I'm going with this?"

Buffy's mind worked quickly. "Mr. Giles!" she burst out.

"What?"

"He asked me to get a book for him," Buffy explained. "From the store, 'cause I have a free period and I'm a big reader—did it mention that on my transcripts?"

Mr. Flutie stared at her. "Mr. Giles."

"Ask him."

But Mr. Flutie stepped around her, closed the gate, and locked it, fussing the whole time.

"Well, maybe that's how they do things in Britain; they've got that royal family and all kinds of problems. But here at Sunnydale nobody leaves campus while school's in session. Are we clear?"

Buffy kept her face pleasant. "We're clear."

"That's the Buffy Summers I want in my school. The sensible girl, with her feet on the ground."

The principal smiled before he turned and walked away.

For a brief moment Buffy gazed down at her feet. Then she took a leap, sailed easily over the fence, and landed nimbly on the other side.

She threw one quick look back over her shoulder.

And then she ran.

* * *

Willow and Xander left the library and went out into the hall. The bell had rung and students were already filing into their classes.

"Murder, death, disaster," Willow mumbled, making a list in her notebook as they walked. "What else?"

"Paranormal, unexplained." Xander thought a minute, then asked, "You got natural disasters?"

Willow gave him a nod. "Earthquake, flood . . ."

"Rain of toads."

"Right."

"Rain of toads." Xander's tone bordered on disbelief. "Are they really gonna have anything like that in the paper?"

"I'll put it on the search. If it's in there, it'll turn up. Anything that'll lead us to vampires."

Xander looked grumpy. "And I, meanwhile, will help by standing around like an idiot."

"Not like an idiot," Willow soothed him. "Just standing. Buffy doesn't want you getting hurt." She cast him a sidelong glance, then added in a much smaller voice, "I don't want you getting hurt."

They'd reached Willow's class. The two of them stood side by side outside the door.

"This is just too much," Xander sighed. "Yesterday my life is like, 'Oh, no. Pop quiz.' Today—rain of toads."

"I know," Willow agreed, looking around at all the other students. "And everyone else thinks it's just a normal day."

"Nobody knows. It's like we've got this big secret."

"We do. That's what a secret is. When you know something other guys don't."

Her gentle sarcasm was totally lost on Xander. "Right," he said. "Well, you better get to class."

"You mean 'we.' 'We' should get to class."

"Yeah."

"Buffy will be okay," she reassured him. "Whatever's down there, I think she can handle it."

"Yeah, I do, too."

"So do I."

But deep in their hearts, neither of them really believed it.

Chapter 14

Buffy made her way through the graveyard once more, back to the mausoleum.

Except for the feeble light angling in from the doorway, it was just as dark in here as it had been the past night, and Buffy moved cautiously, inching farther and farther into the gloom. Her eyes kept a continual watch. Every sense warned her that a presence lurked nearby, but the shadows closed thick about her, revealing nothing.

She reached the iron door on the opposite side of the room. She tried it, but it was locked. Standing there, she lowered her arms to her sides and let out a long, slow breath. Without turning around, she said, "I don't suppose you've got a key on you?"

For a moment, no one answered.

And then her mysterious "friend" stepped from the shadows, a faint smile in his eyes.

"They really don't like me dropping in," he answered.

"Why not?"

"They really don't like me."

Buffy couldn't help her sarcasm. "How could that possibly be?"

"I knew you'd figure out this entryway sooner or later," he said, changing the subject. "Actually, I thought it was gonna be a little sooner."

"I'm sorry you had to wait," Buffy retorted. "Look, if you're gonna be popping up with this cryptic wise-man act on a regular basis, can you at least tell me your name?"

Another silence. Then, "Angel."

"Angel." She waited for a last name. When he didn't respond, Buffy added somewhat offhandedly, "It's a pretty name."

"Don't go down there." The warning was calm, matter-of-fact. Buffy shrugged it off.

"Deal with my going."

"You shouldn't be putting yourself at risk. Tonight is the Harvest. Unless you can prevent it," his voice dropped to a whisper, "the Master walks."

Stubbornly Buffy held her ground. "If this Harvest thing is such a suckfest, why don't *you* stop it?"

"Because I'm afraid."

It was an answer she hadn't expected and wasn't the least prepared for. The unashamed openness of his confession caught her completely off guard. She stared at him, at his face silhouetted in the dim light.

She kicked the door open.

"They'll be expecting you," Angel said.

"I've got a friend down there—or a potential friend." Almost as an afterthought, Buffy joked, "Do you know what it's like to have a friend?"

Angel didn't answer. Buffy paused, a note of gentleness creeping into her voice.

"That wasn't supposed to be a stumper," she told him.

"When you hit the tunnels, head east, toward the school. That's where you're likely to find them."

"You gonna wish me luck?"

Again Angel was silent. Buffy gazed at him, then turned abruptly and headed into the darkness.

Angel watched her go.

He stood there for a long while without moving, and his face held quiet concern.

"Good luck," he said softly.

Chapter 15

The tunnels spread like a forbidden maze beneath the city. Dark and twisting, they ran in all directions, and as Buffy made her way carefully down a flight of steps, she wondered if she'd ever find her way out again.

She stood for a moment, taking in her surroundings. Damp, fetid air washed over her, and there was a faraway echo of dripping water. When a rat scurried across her foot, Buffy didn't even flinch. Instead she squared her shoulders, chose one tunnel, and started down.

She moved slowly, her senses groping into every crack and crevice, through every thick bank of shadows. It was a perfect breeding ground for the undead, she thought grimly—and she knew they could be anywhere at all, watching her, waiting. With the murky blackness flowing over her, she continued along the tunnel, heart pounding wildly in her chest.

She came to a corner and turned. This new passageway seemed to be empty, but still she hesitated a moment longer, ears straining through the eerie quiet. Once more she started forward, every nerve on edge.

She thought she heard something then. Spinning around, she sneaked back the way she'd come and peered around a wall into yet another tunnel.

Shadows, but nothing more. A vague hum of indistinct noise, but nothing she could really identify.

Buffy pulled her head back . . .

And realized he was standing behind her.

For one horrible instant she froze. Her body tensed, prepared for attack, and she whirled around, right into a familiar face.

"Did you see anything?"

"Xander!" Buffy exploded. "What are you doing here?"

"Something stupid. I followed you," Xander didn't seem at all contrite. "I couldn't just sit around not doing anything."

Buffy stared at him, not knowing whether to laugh or scream. "I understand. Now go away."

"No!"

"Xander, you're gonna have to!"

"Jesse's my bud, okay?" Xander insisted. "If I can help him, then that's what I gotta do."

She paused, weighing the sincerity of his words.

"Besides," Xander added, "it's this or chem class."

Buffy sighed.

Without further argument, they continued down the tunnel, reaching the end and pausing to listen.

There was nothing around the next corner.

Relieved, they turned into still another passageway, their eyes searching the shadows. They kept close to each other, bodies tense, ready for anything.

"Okay," Xander said, trying to prepare himself. "So, crosses, garlic, stake through the heart."

"That'll get it done," Buffy assured him.

"Cool. Of course, I don't actually have any of those things."

Buffy gave him a look, then immediately handed him a cross. "Good thinking."

"Well, the part of my brain that would tell me to bring that stuff is still busy telling me not to come down here," Xander defended himself. "I brought this, though."

He produced a flashlight and flicked it on. The bright beam of light stabbed through the darkness, illuminating seeping walls and oozing puddles underfoot.

"Turn that off!" Buffy hissed while Xander scrambled to do so.

"Okay, okay," Xander complied. "So, what else?"

"What else what?"

"For vampire slayage."

Buffy sighed. "Fire, beheading, sunlight, holy water . . . the usual."

"So," Xander's voice sounded a little weak. "You've done some beheading in your time?"

"Oh, yeah. There was this one time, I was pinned down by this vampire, he played left tackle for the varsity—I mean, before he was . . . well anyway, he's got one of those really thick necks, and all I've got is a little X-Acto knife—"

She broke off abruptly as Xander gaped at her.

"You're not loving this story," she accused him.

Xander managed to suppress a shudder. "Actually," he mumbled, "I find it oddly comforting."

CHAPTER 16

In the library, Giles was on a quest of his own.

With his ancient texts spread out upon the table, he looked closely from one to another, reading passages, pondering their various meanings. He'd been at it for some time now, and the look on his face was weary but still determined. He picked up yet another of his volumes, consulted it, and suddenly discovered something quite interesting.

Giles peered closely at one particular passage. And then he began to translate it aloud, softly to himself, from the original Latin.

"'For they will gather, and be gathered. All that is theirs shall be his. . . . From the Vessel pours life.'" Giles paused, repeating thoughtfully, "Pours life . . ."

He studied the engraving on the facing page of his book. The picture showed a hideous man-beast with his hand extended, commanding a throng of villagers. All of the villagers were bleeding. Below them, in what might have been hell, a demon glowed with power.

Giles leaned closer. His brow furrowed in concentration.

Upon the bestial one's forehead, a crude symbol had been drawn. A star with three points.

Giles squinted behind his glasses, peering intently at yet another passage. Once more he began to read.

"'On the night of the crescent moon, the first past the solstice, it will come.'"

He straightened up. Realization dawned upon his face.

"Of course," he mumbled. "Tonight."

"Are we going to the Bronze tonight?" Harmony asked Cordelia.

They were in computer class—definitely not one of Cordelia's favorites. And today—like all other days—even though everyone else was working diligently on their assignments, devising programs was the furthest thing from Cordelia's mind.

Now she glanced over at Harmony, her class partner, who was also struggling to make sense of their project, and Harmony realized that Cordelia hadn't heard her question.

"No!" Cordelia burst out in total frustration. "It's supposed to find the syntax and match it. Or, wait . . ."

Harmony kept her eyes on the keyboard, typing

slowly. "Are we going to the Bronze tonight?" she asked again.

"No," Cordelia retorted. "We're going to the other cool place in Sunnydale."

Harmony gave her a blank look, and Cordelia sighed.

"Of course we're going to the Bronze! Friday night, no cover. But you should have been there last night."

Harmony didn't ask what had happened. Instead she just frowned at their program. "I think we did this part wrong."

"Why do we have to devise these programs?" Cordelia asked irritably. "Isn't that what nerds are for?" She glanced at the desk beside them where Willow was sitting. "What did *she* do?" she mumbled.

Harmony craned over to look at Willow. The girl was obviously lost in her own world, whatever that could possibly be. She was bringing things up on the Net and was completely engrossed in her work, typing intently, scrolling, and searching for God knew what . . .

Harmony shrugged and looked at Cordelia. "Uh, she's doing something else."

Cordelia glared. Sure enough, the nerd girl was busy at the next terminal, her forehead creased in total concentration. Cordelia dismissed her with a sneer and went back to holding court.

"Okay," she said to Harmony, trying halfheartedly to focus on their assignment. "And then 'Pattern Run,' right? Or 'Go To End.' That's it."

Harmony looked completely lost. "Maybe . . . I think . . ."

"Well, what does the book say?" Cordelia was practically out of patience. As Harmony looked up the procedure, Cordelia tried once more to interest her in some gossip. "So anyway," she went on, "I come out of the bathroom and she comes running at me with a stick, screaming, 'I'm gonna kill you! I'm gonna kill you!' I swear."

"Who?" Jared asked. He was one of the cutest guys in class, and he leaned eagerly from his desk now to listen.

With smug satisfaction Cordelia realized she'd finally hooked an audience.

"Buffy," she told him.

"The new girl," Harmony echoed.

Jared looked puzzled. "What's her deal?"

"She's crazed!" Cordelia said.

"Did you hear about her old school?" Harmony asked conspiratorily. "Booted."

"I exhibit no surprise," Cordelia declared.

Jared leaned closer. "Why was she kicked out?"

"'Cause she's a psycholoony," Cordelia said.

"No, she's not."

The voice was totally unexpected. It spoke out firmly and calmly, and the other three turned to look.

Willow sat staring at them. Cordelia stared back.

No one—*no* one—*ever* contradicted Cordelia, and it took an endless moment for the reality of the situation to actually sink in.

"What?" Cordelia leveled her with an icy gaze.

"She's not a psycho," Willow said. "You don't even know her."

Cordelia's voice rose indignantly. "Excuse me? Who gave you permission to exist? Do I horn in on your private discussions? No. Why? Because you're boring."

Hurt flashed in Willow's eyes. She lowered them quickly, then stood and gathered some pages that had come up on the printer. Cordelia and the others turned back to their projects.

"There." Harmony sounded relieved. "I think the program's done."

Cordelia nodded. "Finally the nightmare ends. Now how do we save it?"

Willow was just going out the door. She glanced back and said, "Deliver."

"Deliver." Cordelia stared at the screen. "Where is that—oh!"

She spotted the key marked DEL. She tapped it smartly with one finger.

There was a long pause.

Cordelia and Harmony kept their eyes upon the computer screen. They watched as their program faded, then melted away . . . while their own smiles melted into utter bewilderment.

Chapter 17

"They're close," Buffy said.

They'd been walking quite a while without speaking. Tunnel after tunnel melted into nothingness behind them, and their uneasiness continued to grow. There was no comfortable banter between them now. The air was heavy, thick with a dark, dangerous expectancy, and Buffy frowned as she scanned the blackness with worried eyes.

"How can you tell?" Xander asked nervously.

"No more rats."

It wasn't exactly the information he wanted to hear, but Xander said nothing. They passed through several more tunnels before he spoke again.

"Over there." He stopped, pointing. "What's that?"

Ahead of them was a small, gloomy side chamber.

They could just barely make out the outline of a doorway, but past that, nothing.

After a quick glance behind them, the two walked closer. Xander pulled out his flashlight and played it slowly over the entrance.

The light shone faintly just beyond the opening. Over the motionless shape of a body, lying facedown on the ground.

Xander drew a quick, sudden breath. "Jesse!"

"Oh, no . . ." Buffy murmured.

She started forward as Xander kept the light focused on her. Reaching Jesse, she held out her arms to help him.

Jesse leaped at her without warning, a heavy pipe brandished in his fist. As he prepared to bring it down on her head, Xander's voice rang out.

"Jesse!"

Jesse stopped, amazed. "Xander?"

With a look of sheer relief, Jesse dropped his weapon. He walked slowly toward his friend, meeting Xander's hug with one of his own. After a moment, Xander pulled away, holding Jesse at arm's length, looking him over.

"Jesse, man, are you okay?"

"I'm not okay on an epic scale." Jesse made a frail attempt at humor. "We gotta get out of here!"

He pointed to his leg. A heavy chain held him fast to a metal ring in the wall.

"It's cool!" Xander assured him. "Buffy's a superhero!"

At the mention of her name, the superhero frowned and ran one hand along Jesse's restraints.

"Hold on," she said grimly.

Taking the pipe he'd dropped, Buffy smashed the lock on the shackles. The sound of it reverberated back and back through the labyrinth of tunnels, and Xander cringed, fixing her with a doubtful stare.

"You think anybody heard that?" he murmured.

From the corner of her eye Buffy thought she saw something moving just outside the chamber door . . . several black indistinct shapes shifting within the shadows.

She motioned the others to follow her out.

"They knew you were gonna come," Jesse told her anxiously. "They said that I—I was the bait . . ."

"Oh, now you tell us," Xander grumbled.

"I've seen their leader," Jesse went on. He didn't have to elaborate; as Buffy and Xander watched him, the look of sheer horror in his eyes said all there was to say.

Quickly Buffy led the way back through the tunnel. Then without warning, she froze in her tracks.

Xander and Jesse could see them now, too. The deep, murky, shadowy things moving at the other end of the passageway . . .

"Oops," Buffy said.

Jesse's voice quivered with fear. "Oh, no, no . . ."

"Do you know another way out?"

Jesse threw her a desperate look. "I don't, uh, maybe?"

"Come on," Xander ordered.

Turning, the three of them hurried in the opposite direction. They began to run, and as they came to a junction of several tunnels, they chose one and headed inside. They didn't expect to see the eyes there ahead of them, gleaming in the darkness—they didn't expect the whispered sounds of laughter. In rising panic they swung back again, until they reached yet another intersection.

"Wait, wait," Jesse paused breathlessly. "They brought me through here! There should be a way up. I hope."

No one stopped to argue—they simply ran.

A moment later they found themselves in a small, murky chamber. Too late, they saw the vampires closing slowly in behind them—too late, they realized there was no other way out. In mounting horror, Buffy and Xander looked around for an escape, but there was nowhere to go.

Buffy raced back to the doorway. She could hear the vampires stalking closer and closer, and she glanced frantically at her friends. "I don't think this is the way out!"

"We can't fight our way back through those things," Xander's voice was shaking as much as her own. "What do we do?"

"I've got an idea," Jesse said.

He was standing right behind Xander.

But as the other two turned to look at him, he wasn't Jesse anymore.

His face was repulsive and twisted, an inhuman

face, an unholy face. His eyes were cold and passionless, and as he smiled at them, his pointed teeth gleamed through the darkness.

Buffy and Xander were too shocked to answer. As they stared at him helplessly, Jesse's smile widened.

"You can die."

Chapter 18

In painfully slow motion, Xander began backing away from Jesse, while Buffy's mind raced, trying to think what to do. As she glanced at Jesse, then back again to the doorway, she could hear the vampires closing in on them, could see their shadows slithering along the outside walls.

"Jesse . . ." Xander tried to appeal to him. "Man, I'm sorry . . ."

Jesse regarded him with a triumphant sneer. "Sorry? I feel good, Xander. I feel strong."

Even as they talked, Buffy was grabbing at the door, trying desperately to shut it—but the thick metal had rusted badly, jamming it open.

"I'm connected, man," Jesse slowly advanced on Xander. "To everything. I can hear the worms in the earth."

Xander managed a weak nod. "Well, that's a plus."

"I know what the Master wants. I'll serve his purpose. That means you die. And I feed."

"Xander!" Buffy shouted. "The cross!"

Xander didn't hesitate. Gripping it tightly, he thrust the cross in front of Jesse's face. Jesse stopped in his tracks. His ugly smile began to fade.

With all her strength, Buffy pushed against the door. At last she could feel it giving way beneath her, ever so slightly—but she could also hear the vampires, their measured footfalls, their muffled laughter along the passageway. They were practically at the entrance now, and in the flickering shadows she caught quick glimpses of their fiendish grins. They were certain of their victory. It was only a matter of seconds.

"Jesse." Xander tried again. "Man, we're buds. Can't you remember?"

"You're like a shadow to me now," Jesse snarled.

Xander moved toward him, cross in hand. "Then get out of my face!"

Jesse was furious. He stumbled backward as Xander forced him toward the doorway.

With a last-ditch effort, Buffy heaved at the door. She could see the vampires massed together in the corridor. Getting nearer . . . nearer . . .

Jesse lashed out, knocking the cross from Xander's grasp. He grinned victoriously—but only for an instant. Without warning Buffy grabbed him from behind and hurled him out of the room, knocking vampires over like so many bowling pins. Xander stood staring in disbelief.

"Help me!" Buffy cried.

Recovering himself, Xander rushed to her aid. The two of them wedged their backs against the door, straining for all they were worth. At last there was a slow groan of loosening metal—and then—blessedly—the door slammed shut.

The arm shot in without warning.

Groping and grasping for their faces, trying to pull them out.

Buffy jerked the door open slightly, then slammed it again till the arm withdrew. This time she managed to bolt the door, and as she did so, she turned to look at Xander.

He was as breathless as she was. Still stunned over what had happened to Jesse. "I can't believe it . . . we were too late."

A resounding thud shuddered the door behind them. The vampires were trying to break it down.

"We need to get out of here," Buffy said grimly.

"There *is* no out of here!"

Another thud shook the door to its very frame. Horrified, Buffy could see it beginning to buckle on its hinges. She glanced around, mind working swiftly. There were odds and ends of assorted junk lying about the room, and she started picking them up, flinging them away, searching for some other route of escape.

Xander was also scanning the area. As his eyes darted quickly over the walls, he suddenly spied something high up in the shadows. It looked like an air vent. Just a hint of grating behind a metal sheet, practically obscured by the darkness.

"What's that?" he asked, getting Buffy's attention.

Buffy looked, too. She threw down a box she was holding, then used it as a footstool to try and reach the vent. She peeled away the sheet of metal, revealing the grate behind it. Her heart gave a hopeful leap.

It was indeed an air vent.

And it was big enough to climb through.

Using her bare hands, Buffy tried to pry open the grate. She tried to shut out the sounds of the vampires behind them, the thudding and pounding, the screech of breaking hinges . . .

Xander glanced worriedly from Buffy to the door. It was off its hinges now, he could see—just enough for a vampire to put his fingers through, just enough for a vampire to get a really good grip—

Buffy ripped the grating loose and flung it aside.

"Come on!" she shouted.

A vampire shot out of the air vent. Its rotting arm came straight at her, and the scaly fingers closed around her head.

Behind them, the door burst wider. A vampire's face squeezed through, grinning at them in smug triumph.

Buffy yanked the vampire out of the vent and

hurled him to the floor. She jumped down on top of the creature, pinning him, and yelled at Xander, "Go!"

Xander didn't argue. He raced past her and climbed up on the box just as Buffy sank a stake into the vampire's back. Fumbling the flashlight, Xander aimed it into the vent.

Empty. The vent seemed clear, at least for now.

With one last look at Buffy, Xander crawled inside the vent and began worming his way toward safety.

In the distance, he could hear a muffled crash as the door broke down at last. He could hear the vampires piling into the room.

At the last possible second, Buffy jumped up, clawing at the wall.

Then she pulled herself into the air vent and hurried after Xander, with the vampires close behind.

Crawling on all fours in the darkness, Buffy and Xander were aware of the creatures following, squeezing their rotting bodies one by one into the narrow air vent, keeping close on their trail.

They had no idea how far they'd gone, but suddenly the tunnel opened into a much wider space, and the two of them spotted a ladder leading up. High above them, the faintest glow of sunshine showed through a grating at the top.

Xander glanced over his shoulder at Buffy. "Up?"

"UP!"

He started climbing, Buffy right behind him. Reaching the top, he opened the grating, then hoisted himself out onto the deserted street. He turned at once to help Buffy. His hand closed tightly around hers, and he began pulling her free.

She'd almost cleared the opening when something grabbed her. She felt the scaly, pointed fingers clamp around her ankle as the vampire tried to drag her back into the hole.

Instinctively, Buffy strained upward. With Xander's arms tight around her, she pulled harder, forcing the hand into the afternoon sunlight. The fingers began to smoke, and there was a horrible stench of burning flesh. After an agonizing shriek, the hand twisted back into the darkness and Buffy rolled out, slamming the grate shut.

She lay on the ground beside Xander.

Neither of them spoke and neither of them moved.

They only lay there, side by side, stunned and shaken, trying to catch their breath.

Chapter 19

The Master rose slowly and silently from his chair. His face was grim and his eyes were dangerously hard.

Several vampires stood uneasily before him and he took his time with them, toying with their fear, allowing his pitiless gaze to linger upon each one in turn.

"She escaped," the Master spoke at last. "She walks free when I should be drinking her heart's blood right now. Careless."

The vampire called Colin at last found the courage to speak. "Master, we had her trapped," he tried to explain, but the Master stopped him with a glance.

"Are you going to make excuses?" the Master hissed. "You are all weak. It's been too long since you faced a Slayer." He considered a moment, then added, "But it's no matter to me. She'll not stop the Harvest. It just means there will be someone worth killing when I reach the surface."

He took a step closer to Colin. He leaned down into Colin's face.

"Is Luke ready?" the Master asked.

Colin nodded. "He waits."

The Master seemed pleased at this. He gestured vaguely to another vampire who kept his head lowered.

"It's time," the Master said. "Bring him to me." Then, almost as an afterthought, "And Colin, you failed me." His voice purred with gentle malice. "Tell me you're sorry."

Colin felt a stab of fear. "I'm sorry . . ." he whispered.

"There, now." The Master nodded. "That wasn't so hard. Oh, hold on—"

He jabbed his finger viciously into Colin's face. Colin gasped in pain as his eyeball suddenly popped, squishing deep in its socket.

The Master smiled at him. "You've got something in your eye."

Chapter 20

Giles was still poring intently over his notes. When he suddenly realized that someone had entered the library, he glanced up, his voice hopeful.

"Buffy?"

Willow shook her head, looking apologetic. "It's just me. So there's no word?"

Giles's face fell. "Not as yet." He looked very tired as he took off his glasses.

"Well, I'm sure they're . . . great," Willow offered, trying to reassure herself as much as him.

"Did you find anything of interest?" he asked her.

The girl sat down, spreading out the copied articles so he could see.

"I think maybe. I looked through the old papers, around the time of that big earthquake back in 'Thirty-seven." Willow placed her finger on one of the pages. "And for several months before it, there was a rash of murders."

"Great!" Giles straightened and put his glasses back on. "I mean, not great in a good way. . . . Go on."

Willow obligingly began flipping through the articles. "They sound like the kind you were looking for. Throats, blood. Months, and not even a clue."

"It's all coming together." He nodded. And then, with an anxious glance at Willow, "I rather wish it weren't."

The time was drawing nearer.

The Harvest was at hand.

Darla lit the last row of candles at the back of the church. Solemnly she stepped away from them, clutching her taper, and at the exact moment, another vampire completed his own row of lighted candles along the opposite wall. The flickering light cast a strange, sickly glow over the congregation. The two lines of candles extended all the way to the altar, to the place where their Master stood waiting.

The chanting had begun again. Yet not quite a chanting . . . more a low, primal whisper that made the blood turn cold . . .

Luke stepped forward and drew off his shirt. He stepped forward to the altar and knelt humbly before his Master. When the Master held out his hand Luke kissed it, and when the Master turned his open palm upward Luke kissed that as well.

And then very gently, Luke took hold of the Master's wrist. He lifted it delicately to his mouth, and he sank his teeth deep into the arteries and veins.

The Master winced. He shut his eyes and felt centuries of time flowing through him. As Luke continued to feed, he reared back his head in an agony of delicious pain.

"My blood runs with yours," the Master said. "My soul is your province."

"My body is your instrument," Luke murmured.

Luke pulled away. The Master took one drop of blood from his own wrist, then touched it to Luke's forehead, painting a three-pointed star.

He faced his disciples and spoke.

"On this most hallowed night, we are as one. Luke is the Vessel. Every soul he takes shall feed me. Their souls will grant me the power to free myself."

A smile spread across his face. His eyes narrowed with keen anticipation.

"Tonight I will walk the earth . . . and the stars themselves will hide."

Buffy and Xander dragged themselves wearily into the library. As Giles and Willow stared open mouthed at their disheveled appearance, it was painfully obvious that nothing good had come of their search. Still, Willow couldn't help asking.

"Did you find Jesse?" she asked, though deep down she was pretty sure she already knew the answer.

Xander confirmed it with a terse reply. He wouldn't even look at her. "Yeah."

"Worse," Buffy echoed.

She plopped heavily into a chair, her face a mixture of anger and regret.

"I'm sorry, Willow," she said. "We were too late. And they were waiting for us."

Willow shook her head. "At least you two are okay."

"I don't like vampires," Xander burst out. He aimed his foot at a trash can, kicking it in frustration. "I'm gonna take a stand and say they're not good."

Buffy turned to the Watcher. "So, Giles, you got anything that can make this day worse?"

"How about the end of the world?" he replied calmly.

"I knew I could count on you."

"This is what we know," Giles went on. "Some sixty years ago, a very old, very powerful vampire came to this shore, and not just to feed."

Buffy sat down at the table. She rested her chin on her hands. "He came 'cause this town is a mystical whoosit?"

"Yes. The Spanish who first settled here called it Boca Del Infierno—roughly translated: Hellmouth." Giles began pacing. "A sort of portal from this reality to the next. This vampire hoped to open it."

"Bring the demons back."

"End of the world," Xander clarified.

"But he blew it," Willow picked up the story. "Or, I mean, there was an earthquake that swallowed about half the town. And him, too—or at least there were no more vampire-type killings afterward."

Giles looked thoughtful as he pulled up a chair. "Opening dimensional portals is tricky business. Odds are he got himself stuck. Like a cork in a bottle."

"And this Harvest thing is to get him out?" Xander asked.

"It comes once in a century. On this night."

Giles stood and crossed to a chalkboard where he'd rendered several mysterious diagrams. He began to design several more as he explained.

"A Master can draw power from one of his minions while it feeds. Enough power to break free and to open the portal. The minion is called the Vessel, and he bears this symbol."

He paused, pointing to a sketch of the three-pointed star.

"So," Buffy made an attempt at cheerfulness. "I dust anyone sporting this look, and no Harvest."

"Simply put," Giles responded, "yes."

"Any clue where this little get-together is being held?"

"Well, there are a number of possibilities—"

Before Giles could finish, Xander broke in. "They're going to the Bronze."

The room went silent. They all stared at him.

"Are you sure?" Willow looked surprised, but Xander simply shrugged his shoulders.

"Come on, tasty young morsels all over the place. Anyway, that's where Jesse's gonna be. Trust me."

"Then we need to get there." Giles's voice was tense. "The sun will be down before long."

The four of them headed out the door, but Buffy suddenly turned in another direction.

"I gotta make a stop," she explained. "Won't take long."

"What for?" Giles asked.

Buffy gave a secretive smile. "Supplies."

Chapter 21

Dusk was already beginning to fall.

The last bloodred rays of sunlight streamed through Buffy's window, and the round ball of sun eased itself lower upon the horizon.

"Buffy?" Joyce Summers called from the hallway.

Buffy heard her, but she didn't respond. She just kept rummaging through her closet as her mother finally entered the bedroom. *If you are born to be a Slayer,* Buffy reasoned, *you have to look the part—you can't wear just any old outfit to the Harvest . . .*

The brown jacket, she decided. The leather one. *Definitely.*

"You're going out?" her mother asked, standing behind her.

Buffy heard the frown in her mom's voice. She tried to keep her own tone casual.

"I have to."

There was a pause. Then her mother said just as casually, "I didn't hear you come in last night."

Buffy thought quickly. "I was quiet."

This time the silence wasn't pleased. And it bordered dangerously on disappointment. "It's happening again, isn't it?" Joyce sighed.

Buffy stopped rummaging. She straightened up, turned, and fixed her mother with a level gaze.

"I got a call from your new principal," Joyce went on. "Says you missed some classes today."

"I was . . . running an errand."

Buffy smiled briefly and turned back to the closet. She pulled out an old trunk, opened it, and began going through the contents. She could feel her mother's eyes boring into her back.

"We haven't finished unpacking, and I'm getting calls from your principal," Joyce worried.

"Mom, I promise you, it's not gonna be like before." An edge of desperation crept into Buffy's voice. "But I have to go."

"No."

Buffy couldn't believe what she was hearing. "Mom . . ."

She glanced up at the window, at the thickly spreading darkness. Joyce awkwardly stood her ground.

"The tapes all say I should get used to saying it," she explained to Buffy, sounding almost defensive. "No."

"This is really, really important," Buffy said pleading.

"I know. You have to go out or it'll be the end of the world. Everything is life or death when you're a sixteen-year-old girl."

"Mom, I don't have time to talk about it—"

"You've got all night, Buffy. You're not going anywhere. Now you can stay up here and sulk if you want. I won't hold it against you." Joyce took a deep breath and put both hands on her daughter's shoulders. "But if you want to come down, I'll make us some dinner."

She left, closing the door quietly but firmly behind her. Buffy stared after her for a moment, then shook her head and reached down into the trunk.

All her special things were in there—photographs, letters, her diary, mementoes from her childhood, a *Teen Beat* magazine . . .

She groped along the bottom, then lifted it out. No one but she knew that the trunk had a false bottom. And no one but she knew about the secret cache that lay beneath it—the stakes and crosses, the host, the garlic, the widemouthed jar of holy water. Quickly she gathered everything up and stuffed them into a bag.

Then, almost reverently, Buffy withdrew one particularly deadly looking stake. It fit in her hand as if it were part of it, a normal extension of her arm. This she slid carefully up into her sleeve.

She got up and went to the door.

She pressed her ear flat against the wood. For a long moment she stood there and listened.

Then she tiptoed to the window and opened it.

And crawled out into the night.

Chapter 22

"Senior boys are the only way to go," Cordelia said with practiced ennui.

She was holding court again—this time at the Bronze—and her groupies were gathered adoringly about her at their table on the balcony.

"They're just a better class of person," Cordelia went on. "The boys in our grade? Forget about it. They're children. Like Jesse—did you see him last night?" She rolled her eyes in half amusement, half disgust. "The way he follows me around . . . he's just like a little puppy dog—you just want to put him to sleep."

She leaned forward, eyes wide with superiority.

"Senior boys have mystery, they have . . . what's the word I'm searching for? *Cars.*"

Beside her, Raine started to speak. Cordelia instantly interrupted.

"I'm just not the type to settle," she explained. "If I go into a clothing store, I always have to have the most expensive thing, not because it's *expensive,* but because it *costs* more."

Again Raine attempted to speak. Again Cordelia cut her off.

"Hello!" Cordelia flashed her a lethal stare. "Miss Motormouth—can I get a sentence finished? Oh! I love this song!"

With friends in tow, she jumped up and headed down the stairs. Within minutes she was dancing away into the middle of the crowd, smugly conscious of the male stares upon her—not to mention the envious glares from the female population. She knew she looked fantastic.

At the door Jesse walked in, but not the Jesse that Cordelia had once known—and loathed.

This Jesse was a new man.

There was a cool, subtle swagger in his step—a look of supreme confidence in his eyes.

His gaze went straight to Cordelia.

And he smiled.

Outside the entrance to the Bronze, things were relatively quiet. A few stragglers lounged against the building, laughing and talking, but the sidewalk was deserted.

At first, no one noticed them coming—the eight shadowy figures strolling leisurely up the street. Their faces were bathed in the dim glow of sputtering streetlights, and none of them said a word.

Not even Luke.

Jesse made his way slowly through the crowds, circling Cordelia, his eyes never leaving her face. She didn't notice him at first. It was the burning intensity of his gaze that finally alerted her, and then when she suddenly realized who it was, she stared at him in surprise.

There was something very different about him.

Something she couldn't quite figure out, but something strangely seductive all the same.

A slow song was playing now.

Cordelia stopped dancing and headed off the floor.

Suddenly he was just there, closer than ever, standing right in front of her, blocking her way. Smiling a vague, knowing smile.

"What do *you* want?" Cordelia demanded.

She wasn't fooling anyone. Not even herself, and certainly not Jesse. Without a word he took her hand and led her back onto the floor.

"Hey!" Cordelia objected. "Hello, caveman-brain! What do you think you're doing?"

He turned to her . . . gave her an irresistible smile.

"Shut up," he said.

She'd never have guessed he was such a great dancer. Guiding her to the center of the floor, Jesse held her and started moving in perfect rhythm, barely touching her, his body suggestive and sensuous.

Cordelia's heart raced wildly. She could feel her resolve beginning to crumble.

"Just this one dance . . ." she murmured, and pressed close to Jesse.

They saw the bouncer before he saw them.

He stood at the front entrance, all authority and muscle, and tried to stop them as they headed for the door.

"I need ID," he told them.

They wouldn't answer and they wouldn't stop. The bouncer wasn't particularly fond of trouble, so he tried raising his voice.

"Hey! Nobody goes inside till I see—"

Luke had no time for threats. He grabbed the bouncer and held him face-to-face, grazing him coldly with his eyes. The bouncer didn't seem quite so brave now. In fact, Luke could feel him shaking.

"Get inside," Luke growled.

Once through the door, the vampires began spreading out, each of them heading for an exit, while two stayed behind to close off the front. Darla took the door that led backstage. Another vampire made his way to the bar, swung himself over, and stood in front of the exit. As another pushed his way toward the balcony, Luke climbed up alone onto the stage.

Darla checked her door once again, making certain it was secure. Then she opened a fuse box on the wall and flipped the switch.

Immediately the main lights and music went off. Surprised gasps and murmurs swept through the crowd, and as everyone looked about in confusion, a voice called out from the front of the room.

"Ladies and gentlemen," Luke announced, "there's no cause for alarm."

A single beam of light still shone onstage. Confident that he had their undivided attention now, Luke stepped into the spotlight and faced the bewildered crowd.

"Actually," his lips twisted in a mockery of a smile, "there is cause for alarm. It just won't do any good."

He saw their expressions of revulsion and disbelief. He felt their waves of weakness and growing panic coursing through his veins. He thrived on it—thrived on *all* of it—it only served to make him stronger.

A terrified couple tried to get out. Luke grinned as the vampire at the door teasingly shook his head at them. His face was as revolting as Luke's, and the couple shrank away.

Cordelia was staring up at the stage, Jesse's hands still on her shoulders.

"I thought there wasn't any band tonight," she said blankly.

She looked back at Jesse, recoiling in horror at the horrible change in him, at the hideous sight of his face. She tried to struggle, but he held her tightly and pulled her back into the darkness beneath the stairs.

It was time.

* * *

"This is a glorious night," Luke proclaimed. His predatory eyes hungrily scanned the sea of faces below him. "It's also the last one any of you shall ever see."

There was a tense, uncomprehending moment of silence.

Then Luke commanded, "Bring me the first!"

He watched, sneering, as the bouncer was thrust onstage.

"What do you guys want?" the young man asked earnestly. "You want money? Man, what's wrong with your faces?"

Luke grabbed him by the scruff of the neck, squeezing any further conversation out of him.

"Watch me, people!" he shouted. And then to the struggling victim in his grasp, "Their fear is elixir. It's almost like blood."

With one expert motion, Luke bit into the young man's neck, sucking his life out in huge, wet gulps. He could feel a warm red haze enveloping him . . . could sense his Master growing stronger and stronger with every sip, the power of the ages coursing through his Master's veins, radiating through him like divine light . . .

Luke continued to feed.

After several moments longer, he pulled his head back and flung the young man's body away.

"Next!" he roared.

Chapter 23

There was no one outside when Buffy and the others finally reached the Bronze. Buffy struggled to get the front door open, but it wouldn't budge.

"It's locked," she told them.

Giles looked almost sick. "We're too late."

"Well, I didn't know I was gonna get grounded!" Buffy almost yelled at him.

"Can you break it down?" Xander asked, but Buffy shook her head.

"Not this thing. You guys try the back entrance. I'll find my own way."

"Right." Giles glanced from Xander to Willow. "Come on."

"Guys!" Buffy called out to them.

The three stopped. Buffy handed them her bag.

"You get the exit cleared, and you get people out,"

she instructed them. "That's all. Don't go Wild Bunch on me."

"See you on the inside," Giles promised.

As they took off around the building, Buffy began circling in the other direction. Her expression was grim and she kept her eyes on the roof above.

It only took a minute for Giles and the others to reach the back. Xander tried the door, but it too was locked. They looked around frantically for something to open it with.

"Damn!" Xander exploded. "We've got to get in there before Jesse does something stupider than usual."

"Xander," Giles stopped him, "Jesse is dead. You have to remember that if you see him." And then in a kinder voice, "You're not looking at your friend. You're looking at the thing that killed him."

The Master was even more powerful now.

His whole being seemed to glow with energy and light, with indomitable strength, with eternal life.

He stepped once more to the mystical wall that confined him. He placed his hands against it and began to push.

Slowly . . . slowly . . . the wall disintegrated at his touch. Very slightly now . . . but soon . . .

"Almost free," he murmured.

He shut his eyes and his voice raged throughout his sanctuary.

"Yes! Give me more!"

* * *

Luke obeyed.

Flushed with power, Luke triumphantly dropped another body and looked about at his hostages.

They were really terrified now, and it exhilarated him to see it. With the two corpses lying before them, the reality—and the utter hopelessness—of their plight had begun to sink in at last, and he could hear screams and pitiful whimpers from the crowd.

In a corner under the stairs, Darla was facing off with Jesse. He still held on to Cordelia, and he was determined not to give her up.

"This one's mine," Jesse challenged her.

Darla had no time for his games. "They are *all* for the Master," she told him, grabbing the stunned girl from his grasp and heading toward the stage.

Jesse paused, disappointed. "I don't get one?"

They didn't notice the upstairs window opening . . . the window by the balcony where an equally oblivious vampire stood with his back to it. No one saw Buffy slip in and no one saw her standing there, sizing up the situation.

"I feel him rising!" Luke shouted. "I need another!"

Buffy stared at the three-pointed star on his forehead.

"The Vessel . . ." she murmured to herself.

But this time the vampire on duty *did* hear her. As he turned and grabbed her, Buffy felt herself being hauled to the middle of the balcony, another potential offering for Luke.

Luke was still unaware of her intrusion. "Tonight

is his ascension," he informed the horrified onlookers. "Tonight will be history at its end! Yours is a glorious sacrifice. Degradation most holy."

He stopped, his evil gaze sliding from one face to another.

"What, no volunteers?" he mocked.

And then Darla emerged, holding Cordelia.

"Here's a pretty one," she said.

"Nooo . . ." Cordelia struggled, but to no avail. As she started to cry, Darla dragged her toward the stage and handed her over to Luke.

The activity had momentarily distracted Buffy's captor. With one quick movement, she slipped from the vampire's grasp and threw him off the balcony. He landed on his back right in front of the stage.

The room plunged into shocked silence.

"Oh, I'm sorry," Buffy said. "Were you in the middle of something?"

Looking up, Luke's face contorted with fury. *"YOU!"*

"You didn't think I'd miss this, did you?" Buffy tossed back at him.

The anger drained from Luke's expression.

His lips curled in a dangerous smile.

"I hoped you'd come," he said.

Chapter 24

The door was open at last.

Wielding a metal pipe, Giles burst through the backstage exit with Xander and Willow close behind.

At the same moment, a vampire rushed Buffy from the side. Grabbing him easily, she tossed him into the hookah pit, where he tried to scramble back up. Buffy did a backward flip, sailed through the hole, and landed on top of a pool table. There was a cue lying there. With one simple handspring, she grabbed it and landed neatly on her feet.

A vampire came at her other side.

Without looking at him, she jammed the cue end into his heart. There was a soft sound of punctured flesh, and when Buffy released the cue it stayed right where it was.

"Okay, Vessel-boy." She stared straight at Luke, challenge flashing in her eyes. "You want blood?"

She stepped forward as the cue rose into the air. It looked curiously like the arm of a guard gate, and in the next second, the vampire's impaled body thudded to the floor.

"I want yours," Luke snarled at her. "Only yours."

"Then come and get it."

Seeing her chance, Cordelia tried to break free of Luke's grasp. He flung her roughly away just as Buffy leaped at him and slammed her fist into his face. Luke was shocked at her strength. He stumbled back in pain.

Almost instantly he came back at her. Buffy ducked and met his face again, this time with a roundhouse kick. She whipped out her stake and took aim, but he blocked her with a blow to her face. Badly hurt now, Buffy skidded into the corner. The stake fell at Luke's feet.

As the crowd panicked and shoved in all directions, the backstage door burst open. Xander stumbled out and nearly fell, but recovered himself at once. He took a quick look around, saw that the immediate vicinity was free of vampires, and instantly began herding people out.

"Come on!" he yelled.

As fast as he could direct them, Xander moved the panicky crowd through the door. Willow and Giles waited backstage to push everyone safely toward the exit.

Luke was closing in.

Buffy kicked him fiercely in the chest, sending him back against the wall. He landed hard, and seeing her chance, she went in for the kill.

Then she spotted Xander.

He was too busy getting people out to notice the vampire at his back.

Buffy turned to the drum kit, kicked the cymbal off its stand, and caught it in midair. The vampire had reached Xander now; she could see Xander's look of fear as the creature grabbed him.

Buffy hurled the cymbal Frisbee style.

Sensing something, the vampire turned, his eyes wide, as the cymbal flew straight at his neck.

Xander heard the slice and ducked away.

His eyes followed the trajectory of the severed head as it sailed across the room.

"Heads up . . ." Xander mumbled.

Buffy barely had time to turn before Luke grabbed her from behind. His arms closed around her and he lifted her in a crushing bear hug.

Xander started toward her, but a shriek stopped him in his tracks. Whirling around, he saw Jesse dragging Cordelia farther below the stairs. As Cordelia screamed and struggled, Jesse threw her to the ground and knelt above her, pinning her with his weight.

"Hold still!" Jesse ordered her. "You're not helping."

Xander came up behind them. He stood looking down, clutching a stake in his hand. He could do it right then, he thought to himself, could end it right then, just plunge the stake through Jesse's back, straight into Jesse's heart . . .

"Jesse, man . . ." Xander begged him. "Don't make me do it."

Jesse looked up. His grin was anything but human. He looked like something from the dregs of a nightmare.

"Buddy . . ." Jesse said.

Buffy twisted uselessly in Luke's grasp. She could feel him squeezing and squeezing—everything around her spinning, fading to black . . .

She coughed and choked, gasped desperately for air. From some distant place she thought she could hear Luke laughing.

"I've always wanted to kill a Slayer," he confessed. He sounded proud and somewhat amused.

And then Buffy heard something else.

Something inside of her beginning to crack.

CHAPTER 25

The panic had reached full proportions now.

Backstage, people were still rushing out, and Giles shouldered his way through them, shouting to Willow.

"Come on! We've got to open the front as well!"

He headed for the door, moving against a current of hysterical people, trying to reach the main room. Darla came out of nowhere, leaping upon him and digging for his throat. Giles tried to use his stake, but it knocked out of his hand as he toppled to the floor.

Xander took a step back as Jesse rose and faced him.

"Jesse, I know there's still a part of you in there," Xander insisted.

Jesse looked exasperated. "Okay, let's deal with

this. Jesse was an excruciating loser who couldn't get a date with anyone in the sighted community! Look at me now! I'm a new man!"

To prove his point, he grabbed Xander and hurled him against the wall. Xander slid back down again and fell in a heap beside Cordelia.

"See," Jesse sighed impatiently. "The old Jesse would have *reasoned* with you."

Giles was no match for Darla.

While Willow dug frantically through Buffy's bag for a weapon, Giles continued to struggle, all too aware that he was losing the battle. Darla held him flat against the floor, and as he stared up at her, her teeth lowered menacingly toward his neck.

"Get off him!" Willow cried.

Darla turned at the sound of Willow's voice. Something wet hit her full in the face, and she realized too late that she'd been doused with holy water.

Screaming, she brought her hands up to her cheeks, smoke pouring from between her fingers.

Giles pushed her off and staggered to his feet, prepared to confront her. But Darla was already stumbling out of the exit, her face a scorched, sizzling mask of agony.

Up on the stage, it looked as if Buffy was losing her own battle.

Her body went limp in Luke's merciless grasp. Her head dangled forward like a rag doll.

Luke looked down at her, smiling. Wild elation rushed through him, and he uttered his humble prayer.

"Master, taste of this and be free."

His lips peeled back . . . mouth opening wide. He lowered his head, leaning in for the kill.

Buffy hit him so hard, he didn't realize what had happened. He felt the back of her head as she rammed it up into his chin, and the unexpected impact nearly knocked him off his feet.

"How'd it taste?" she asked defiantly.

Despite her bravado, she was still weak. She managed to grab the cymbal stand, holding it out like a weapon, and at the same time quickly assessed the stage to try and form another plan.

Then she noticed the window at the back of the stage.

It hadn't been that visible before, because someone had painted the entire windowpane black.

Buffy looked at the window. She looked at Luke.

Jesse picked Xander up again from the floor and shoved him against the wall. He didn't have time for all these interruptions, these old reminders that meant nothing to him now. He glared at this easy prey that had once been a friend, and cold fury etched his new face. "I'm sick of you getting in the way, you know?" he railed at Xander. "Cordelia, she's gonna live forever. You're not."

Mustering his courage, Xander held the stake up

to Jesse's chest. His face was determined, but Jesse could see that it was also very scared.

Jesse couldn't help but taunt him. "Oh, right! Put me out of my misery! You don't have the g—"

His words gagged in his throat. He felt the sharp, quick thrust and looked down at his stomach.

A panic-stricken girl had slammed into him from behind. She'd been trying to escape and had driven him forward, right onto Xander's stake.

Jesse stared at Xander in shocked surprise.

Gasping, dying, he grabbed onto his old friend.

Xander watched stunned as what once had been Jesse disintegrated into a pile of dust.

He scarcely had time to react before two vampires grabbed him.

Buffy swung the cymbal stand at the steadily advancing Luke. He dodged it easily, bestowing her an evil grin in the process.

"You forget," he sneered. "Metal can't hurt me."

Buffy didn't flinch. "There's something you forgot about, too."

She saw his split-second pause—the flicker of doubt on his face.

"Sunrise," she said.

She hurled the stand through the plate-glass window at the back of the stage. Glass shattered everywhere, and as the warm light streamed in over him, Luke screamed and raised his hands to ward it off.

Then he stopped.

His expression was completely baffled.

With lightning quickness, Buffy drove her stake though Luke's back. He arched forward, his massive body twisted in unbearable pain.

"It's in about nine hours, moron," Buffy reminded him.

It was then that Luke realized the light from the window wasn't daylight at all. Only a streetlight, shining in from the deep, safe darkness.

With a gasp of amazement, he stumbled forward.

He could feel his life draining . . . draining . . . and with it the life of his Master. It was as if they were one and the same: Luke staggering across the stage—the Master staggering forward in his lair as all the bright, vibrant energy began draining from him, too. Luke could feel the Master's suffering—his anguish—the Master reaching out, doubling over, just as Luke was doubled over, just as Luke was falling and crumbling to dust . . .

In those last brief seconds of awareness, Luke could see everything ending—centuries of hope, centuries of waiting, the last vestiges of power melting away from the Master as that mighty one fell weakly to his knees and groped blindly for help that would not come . . .

From far away, Luke heard his strangled cry.

"Nooooo . . ." the Master gasped, and as he touched the mystical wall that entrapped him, it was once again too strong to escape. Fury and despair crossed his face as he gazed up at it. A scream of defeat welled up in his throat.

Through a mystical haze, Luke gazed up and saw Buffy standing breathlessly over him.

And then there was nothing more.

Chapter 26

Xander struggled fiercely with his captors.

The two vampires holding him had momentarily shifted their attention. Their eyes were narrowed, focused uneasily on what had been happening on-stage.

They saw Buffy staring down at the spot where Luke's body had been only a moment before. Then they watched as she turned her gaze slowly and deliberately on them.

They regarded her expresssion for one fraction of a second.

Then without a word, they dropped Xander and bolted for the door.

Xander was just picking himself up again when Giles and Willow came out from backstage. He and Buffy met them in the middle of the dance floor.

Giles glanced around, a note of relief in his voice. "I take it it's over."

"Did we win?" Willow was almost afraid to ask.

The four of them looked about at the carnage surrounding them. Most of the crowd had managed to escape by then, but a few still remained, some sitting, some wandering, all of them stunned and silent.

"Well, we averted the apocalypse," Buffy said wearily. "You gotta give us points for that."

She looked over and saw a dazed Cordelia still in a heap on the floor where Jesse had left her. For once, Cordelia had nothing to say.

"One thing's for sure," Xander sighed. "Nothing is ever gonna be the same."

Out in front of the Bronze, vampires were fleeing in panic. As the last of them retreated down the street, Angel stepped quietly from the shadows and stood there alone, gazing after them.

He turned slightly and stared at the entrance to the club.

And then he smiled.

"She did it," he murmured. "I'll be damned."

CHAPTER 27

Contrary to Xander's prediction, the next day dawned as it always did.

And everything looked amazingly normal.

The warm California sunshine enveloped Sunnydale High, and in the fountain quad the routine was exactly the same. Students milled about laughing and talking, and Cordelia held court with her friends.

"Well, I heard it was rival gangs fighting for turf," she said dramatically. She glanced around at all the eager faces, her adoring fans clinging to every word. "Anyway, Buffy totally knew these guys, which is too weird. I can't remember anything too well, but I'm telling you, it was a freak show."

"Oh, I wish I'd been there," one Cordelia-wannabe sighed.

Crossing the quad in the opposite direction, Buffy

and her own friends happened to overhear Cordelia's play-by-play. While Buffy hid a smile, Xander turned to her in exasperated disbelief.

"Well, what exactly were you expecting?" Buffy chided him, while Xander gave an indignant shrug.

"I don't know! Something. The dead *rose!* We should've at least had an assembly."

"People have a tendency to rationalize what they can," Giles reminded him gently as he joined them outside the building, "and forget what they can't."

Buffy nodded in agreement. "Believe me, I've seen it happen."

"Well, I'll never forget it," Willow said emphatically, giving an inward shudder. "None of it."

Giles looked pleased. "Good. Next time you'll be prepared."

"Next time?" Xander sounded suspicious, while Willow echoed, "Next time is why?"

Giles gave them a tolerant smile. "We stopped the Master from freeing himself and opening the mouth of hell. Doesn't mean he'll stop trying. I'd say the fun is just beginning."

"More vampires?" Willow croaked.

"Not just vampires." Giles stopped and turned to face them. His expression was very solemn, even for him. "The next creature we face may be something quite different."

Buffy rolled her eyes. "I can hardly wait."

"We're at a center of mystical convergence here," Giles went on. "We may in fact stand between the earth and its total destruction."

Xander shook his head. "Buffy, this isn't good."

"Well, I gotta look on the bright side," Buffy told them cheerfully. "Maybe I can still get kicked out of school."

She smiled at Giles and started off, the other two hurrying to keep up with her.

"Hey, that's a plan," Xander was agreeable. "'Cause a lot of schools aren't *on* hellmouths."

"Maybe you could blow something up," Willow suggested helpfully. "They're really strict about that."

Buffy considered this with a shrug. "I was aiming for a subtle approach, like excessive not studying."

Watching them go, Giles shook his head.

He arched one eyebrow and settled his glasses more firmly upon his nose.

"The earth is doomed," he sighed.

About the Author

Richie Tankersley Cusick loves to read and write scary books. Richie enjoys writing when it is rainy and gloomy outside, and likes to have a spooky soundtrack playing in the background. She writes at a desk that originally belonged to a funeral director in the 1800s and that she believes is haunted. Halloween is one of her favorite holidays. She decorates the entire house, which includes having a body laid out in state in the parlor, life-size models of Frankenstein's monster, the figure of Death to keep watch, and scary costumes for Hannah and Meg, her dogs. A neighbor told her that a previous owner of the house was feared by all of the neighborhood kids and no one would go to the house on Halloween.

Richie is the author of *Vampire, Fatal Secrets, The Locker, The Mall, Silent Stalker, Help Wanted, The Drifter, Someone at the Door, Summer of Secrets, Overdue, Starstruck,* and the novelization of *Buffy the Vampire Slayer,* in addition to several adult novels for Pocket Books. She lives outside Kansas City, where she is currently at work on her next novel.